Commander Kell 'SM

#3

Escape From Jungle Island

Christopher P.N. Maselli

Harrison House
Tulsa, Oklahoma

Escape From Jungle Island
ISBN 1-57794-151-9
30-0903

Based on the characters created by Kellie Copeland, Win Kutz, Susan Wehlacz and Loren Johnson.

07 06 05 04 03 02 01 00 99 98   10 9 8 7 6 5 4 3 2 1

All Scripture is from the following translations:

King James Version

New International Version, The Holy Bible, New International Version, Copyright © 1973, 1978, 1984 by the International Bible Society. Used by permission of Zondervan Publishing House.

International Children's Bible, New Century Version, copyright © 1986, 1988 by Word Publishing, Dallas Texas 75039. Used by permission.

Published by Harrison House, Inc.
P. O. Box 35035
Tulsa, Oklahoma 74153

Dedication

For anyone who has ever
battled with fear...

And for Kellie Copeland,
for inspiring the commander
dream in each of us...

Contents

Contents

Dear Superkid,

I'm Valerie Rivera, and have I got a story for you. It's a story about what happened to me recently when I went on vacation...or, what I thought would be a vacation. Actually, it turned out to be the adventure of a lifetime.

To give you a little background, you should know that my parents are missionaries on a place called Calypso Island. I grew up on the large island home for the first seven years of my life with the natives, the grass huts and even the dangers. But I'd always made it a point to make sure I didn't go into the jungle alone...little did I know, just a few years later, I'd be forced to go into the jungle alone—and at night, no less. Even though I'd gone through hours of training at Superkid Academy, I never expected to put it all into practice at one time!

Superkid Academy is where I live most of the year with my friends Paul, Missy, Rapper and Alex. We're part of the Blue Squad, which is led by Commander Kellie. Working together, the bunch of us have been on one great adventure after another...and God has always brought us through with victory.

But what happened to me on the island was tougher than anything I've had to face before. What I faced on the island was my greatest fear.

So are you ready for the unexpected? I hope so...because you're about to find out about all the troubling situations—and all the powerful truths—that I discovered!

Valerie

Escape From Jungle Island

"I thought you said this storm had passed!"

"I thought it had!"

The silver SuperCopter, a technologically advanced helicopter powered by air compression, zipped clumsily through the threatening thunderstorm.

Rummmblllle....Sha-powwwww! A bolt of lightning shot directly in front of the craft's darkened front window. The two young, yet experienced pilots made reflexive maneuvers to compensate for the electrical shock.

"Are we even heading in the right direction anymore?!" Eleven-year-old Valerie wasn't as confident in the ship's navigational controls as she had been when she and Rapper had left Superkid Academy nearly seven hours earlier.

"I don't know if we're even on the same *planet* anymore," Rapper shot back. His eyes were intent upon the sky ahead. Valerie was thankful that she had such a great pilot with her. Anyone else, and she would have been even more concerned about the sudden storm.

Any Superkid would agree that Rapper and Valerie were Superkid Academy's two best pilots. And it just so happened that they were on the same squad at the Academy—the Blue Squad—which is why they both had vacation the same week. Each Superkid squad rotates vacation weeks during the year so that the Academy won't be left with more than one missing squad. This week it was the Blue Squad's turn. And Valerie and Rapper had determined to go to sunny Calypso Island for their time off.

With warm beaches, great homemade food and cool breezes, Calypso Island was Valerie's home for the first seven years of her life, before she attended the Academy. Valerie's parents, the Riveras, were missionaries to the many tribes on the island. There were also many other islands nearby, and one day they hoped to reach them, too, with the powerful message of Jesus, the Anointed Savior of the world.

Rapper scratched his head, messing up his spiked, brown hair. His headset moved slightly and he had to quickly shift it back into place. He looked over at Valerie. She wore the same type of headset, with a microphone extending down to her mouth. Her bobbed, brown hair shifted as their craft hit heavy turbulence.

"Val—look at the radar. Can you tell where the storm ends? Let's head to the nearest break in the clouds!"

Valerie looked at the red, blue and green radar. A thin, electronic line swiftly swept around in a circle, updating the radar with every millimeter it passed. The screen was one huge, colorful mass.

"I don't see *any* end to this storm! We'll have to travel farther. But we can do our best to navigate around the most threatening parts of the storm....oh, no."

"What?! Don't say 'oh, no!' Not now, *please!*"

"Rapper, we're going to have to go through this dark blue mass," Valerie shouted, pointing to a spot on the radar. "It's too huge to avoid it in time—besides Calypso Island is directly on the other si—"

ZIP-BOOM! A huge, red beam shot across the front of the SuperCopter. A split second later, something impacted the side of the craft. *"What was that?!"* Suddenly, a control panel on the wall blew out, shooting sparks throughout the tiny cockpit. Valerie leaned to her left to avoid it, but knocked a gear with her knee. The ship swung sharply to the right.

"Val! Turn it back! Turn it back before we flip!"

Valerie grabbed the gear and yanked it back to its home position. The craft rolled with it, setting them back on course.

"What was that?!" Rapper repeated again. "It looked like a laser blast! Who's shooting at us?!"

Valerie looked at the radar. There was nothing on it but the fierce storm. "I have no idea!" she shouted back.

"I don't know if we can take another hit like that! We've got to get down now for repairs!"

"Father God, we thank You for Your consistent protection for us. According to Psalm 91, we say You are our place of safety and protection."

"Amen!" Rapper agreed.

"Hold on—here we go!" shouted Valerie. The radar indicated that their ship was heading straight into the heart of the big, dark blue mass.

Wind rushed, rain poured, thunder rolled and lightning crashed, daring the tiny SuperCopter to face it head-on. The Superkids ran in full force.

Ka-POWWWW! Another bolt of lightning struck across their bow. Valerie could feel her heart beating faster as her forehead broke out in a chilling sweat. "Rapper!"

"I'm working on it!"

Valerie plugged some coordinates into the main computer. It warbled a beep.

ZIP-BOOM! Another huge, red beam shot across the SuperCopter's bow. Rapper dodged it just in time. He rapped, "Someone's firing at us—I'm sure of that/What I don't know is where they're at!"

"I don't see anything, either...Wait!" Valerie peered closer at the radar. "There is something—someone's ship—but it's zipping away now. Whoever it was, they're leaving us at full speed!"

"Good! We don't need any enemies up here!"

Working together, the two adventurers steered through the turbulent sky.

Valerie glanced down at the radar. *Zzzippp!* Valerie blinked noticeably. "Rapper, the radar just went out!"

Rapper slapped the radar screen with his palm. "C'mon! Well, now we don't have a choice—we *have* to land and get this thing fixed or we could end up flying into something!"

"The last I looked, Calypso Island was straight ahead. Drop down and let's see if we can find it."

"Let's see if we can *see* it," Rapper muttered. He pushed the main gear forward, forcing the craft down. Valerie peered through the dense rain, but the sky was gray and hazy.

"There!" Valerie pointed toward a green patch straight ahead. "Those look like tree tops. Let's head toward 'em."

Rapper nodded. Valerie punched more coordinates in the computer and it spat a string of numbers back at her. Valerie huffed. The repair may have been as simple as replacing a fuse, but she couldn't tell. Thunder crashed nearby.

Soon the SuperCopter brushed the tops of tall trees. Valerie squinted tightly, trying to make out any familiar clearings to land in. She couldn't see any. Just trees.

"One thing I know that's for sure, Val/If we can land, we should do it now!" Rapper's knuckles were white from holding on to the controls so tightly.

"I know! I know! How about over there?" Valerie motioned toward a small break in the trees. Rapper quickly shook his head as he dodged the tip of a tall tree.

"Too small—we need more room!" Valerie knew he was right. They needed to land, and fast. And they needed a good amount of area. But where on the island could they be guaranteed a large clearing? Then it hit her.

"Rapper, let's head to the western edge of the island. It's all beach."

"I don't know about landing in the sand, Val..."

"It's either that or the eastern side of the island—of course that's mostly rocks and shark-infested waters."

"I've decided I *like* the idea of landing in the sand!" Rapper pulled to his left and the weary SuperCopter followed. Valerie held on to the edge of her seat as he swept over the expansive jungle forest. She could barely see through the rainy sky.

"*SQUEEEEE!*"

"*AHHHHH!!!*" Rapper jerked the controls hard to the right and then back to the left. The SuperCopter rocked sideways, tossing the Superkids from side to side.

"What was *that?!*" Valerie shouted. Her heart was racing. They'd almost run into something that shot up through the tops of the trees. Something grayish-brown, ugly, squealing and—

"That thing was awfully fat and big/if you ask me, I think it was a pig!" Rapper rapped.

"What's a pig doing in the clouds during a rainstorm!?"

"What's a pig doing in the clouds *anytime?*" The Superkids shook their heads. They had no idea what it had been—it had shot up in front of them so fast—but they knew they didn't want to run into another one.

"There!" Valerie was pointing again, this time to the western horizon. "The beach!"

Rapper zipped forward at full speed and Valerie punched a couple navigational buttons to no avail. The rain still pounded down, but the lightning was finally gone and the thunder was in the distance. They had made it through the worst.

The young pilot soared to the beach and when they arrived, he brought them down immediately. They landed on soft, wet sand, closer to the jungle than Valerie was comfortable with—simply because she didn't want the SuperCopter's blades to nick the beautiful island palms. The ocean tide was in and the shore was shorter than usual. The SuperCopter rocked twice, its weight pressing against the impressionable island sand. Finally, Valerie cut the power and the two Superkids leaned back and relaxed. With the rain still heavy, they wouldn't be going anywhere for a while.

▲   ▲   ▲

Two hours later, the storm was nothing more than soft droplets peppering the windshield of the SuperCopter. After they relayed a quick message to Commander Kellie, letting her know their current situation, Rapper stood up and headed for the door.

"Boy am I glad *that's* over," he admitted. "You'd think someone could forecast the weather correctly by now."

Valerie was on his heels, eager to exit the confined cockpit and get back to some familiar surroundings. She wasn't concerned about the enemy ship coming back to fight. It was heading away too fast—and it would have to run through the storm to catch up with her and Rapper again. As far as the pig in the clouds goes...well, that was something Valerie hoped was just her imagination.

When they got outside, she put her hands on her hips and arched her back, stretching the muscles that had become sore from sitting too long. She smiled into the sky and felt a rush of relief as droplets of mist kissed her face. She took in a deep, island-fresh breath of air. She could feel the cooling effect of the oxygen as it moved into her lungs and then rolled back out as she exhaled.

She looked down and drew a cross in the sand with her blue and white cross-training shoe. She noticed how bright her royal blue jacket appeared in contrast to the wet, off-white sand. As she unzipped her jacket and removed it, her olive green, cotton tank top and stone-washed jeans proved to be the best outfit for the muggy, hot temperatures of the island. Feeling a bit cooler, she tossed her jacket into the open SuperCopter.

Rapper wore bluejeans and athletic shoes also, and he wore a tan T-shirt sporting a pocket monogrammed with the letters "RR." The letters, of course, stood for "Robert Rapfield," but Valerie knew better than to let anyone else know that. Robert preferred to be called "Rapper"—a nickname he picked up when he learned to rap at the early age of 5. He'd always had a knack for rhyming words together. He usually would do it for fun, but sometimes a rhyme would slip out when he was downright nervous, too (like he was only a while earlier).

Rapper hadn't taken time to look at the beautiful beach and jungle forest surrounding them. He was busy fiddling with the SuperCopter's engine. Valerie strolled over to him. She playfully slugged him in the shoulder.

"Hey, Captain," she said warmly, "what are the damages?"

"Well, I have no idea what hit us, but it does look like we were fired at. Check it out." Valerie looked at the burn hole on the side of the SuperCopter. The metal was charred. Another hit in the same area could have sent them plummeting into the ocean.

"Wow! What else?" she wondered.

"Oh, a blown fuse, a clogged air line and a fried wire that goes who knows where—I guess maybe the NAV computer."

"How long do you think it will take to fix?"

"Not long."

"Why don't I fix the fried wire and you get the air line. The fuse either of us could do. That'll only take a sec."

"Thanks, Val, but c'mon. We just got to your home. Go ahead and relax. Only one of us can work in here at a time anyway. I'm chill. Give me a little while and I'll have it fixed."

Valerie tapped his arm. "OK. If you insist. Thank you, sir. I think I'm going to go look for a path to the main camp. I'm not sure where we are exactly—this area isn't familiar to me. When I find it, I'll let you know."

Rapper smiled. "Well, when I'm done, I'm gonna take the 'Copter up and make sure everything works—shouldn't be long."

"OK. See you in a bit."

"Be careful."

"Careful? There's nothing out there to fear," Valerie said flippantly, angling her thumb toward the jungle. "Nothing I haven't dealt with before. I grew up here, remember?"

Excited, Valerie jogged into the jungle forest. Nonetheless, she stayed near the edge. When she was younger, Valerie had been afraid of the jungle. Her fear stemmed from the tales she had heard about pirate ghosts, vampire bats, 45-foot poisonous snakes and bloodthirsty cannibals.

But now that she was older, she had heard something different. Something true. Something real. She had heard the Word of God. And because of it, her faith had grown strong in believing what God said instead of believing fearful tales people promoted.

Brilliant greens and browns surrounded Valerie as she walked near the edge of the jungle. As she strolled, she kept the beach in sight, simply to help her sense of direction. A few steps farther into the dense jungle and it would have been easy to lose all sense of direction and comfort. She was hoping to spot a path or a sign or even a piece of trash to signal that her parents' civilization was near. But she found nothing.

Huge green leaves, hairy tree trunks, hanging vines, glistening cobwebs, clicks, creeks and clacks surrounded her. Birds chirped, distant monkeys whined and insects scampered. The jungle was alive. Valerie stopped to rest a moment. She placed her left hand on a thick tree trunk as she leaned. Wet fibers tickled her palm. She made another cross in the soft ground with her shoe; the mud folded easily at her touch.

The edges of the cross in the mud slowly crumpled down, beginning the natural process of erosion. Valerie thought about her father and mother's commitment to reach the natives around them with God's love. Each and every day, without fail, they ministered to the natives through their lives and teaching. And the message they shared could never erode away—for they shared the uncompromised Word of God.

Valerie hoped that when she fulfilled her dream of being a commander one day, she'd be able to impart God's Word into her cadets—just like her parents did with the natives. And, like her parents' instructions, Valerie's messages from the Word would take root and live on in her cadets' lives. Maybe even like Commander Kellie, the way she lived would speak volumes to her cadets. With God, she believed it was possible. One day.

God, Valerie prayed silently, *I believe like it says in Philippians 1:6 that You'll be faithful to complete the good work You've begun in my life. I'm not looking for fame or recognition...I just want to be used by You. Lord, I am available.*

Valerie's thoughts came to an abrupt halt when she suddenly heard something that sounded like a butterfly fluttering beside her ear. She shook her head and recognized the familiar sound. It was the whir of the SuperCopter's blades. Valerie looked at her watch and dropped her mouth in amazement when she realized she'd been away for nearly an hour and a half. Rapper was getting ready to test fly the vehicle. Imagining that he was most probably concerned, Valerie took off running the way she came.

As she ran, her steps left soft footprints and mud squirted out from beneath her feet. She headed for the beach at full speed, snapping twigs and vines along the way. In just a moment she'd be there.

CRACK! Valerie's left foot caught a branch and she went plummeting to the earth. *SMACK!* Her hands hit first, followed by her body and then her face. Mud splirted around her, covering her whole body with grimy, jungle-floor goo. She felt the wind knocked out of her as she hit. A quick pain shot through her shoulders, chest and stomach from the impact. Her knees felt the hard fall, too. But it didn't stop her.

Valerie pushed herself up seconds later, carefully feeling around for solid footing. She got it and pushed herself halfway up.

Tss-ss-ss-ss-ss-ss-ss...Valerie heard the SuperCopter lift off.

No...

Wait...

That sound wasn't the SuperCopter.

That sound was coming from directly in front of her. She brought her head up slowly and faced it. Eye to eye.

The tropical rattlesnake was intricately coiled within itself, half buried in leaves, staring at her. Valerie felt her legs go weak, but didn't move a muscle. Drops of muddy water trickled off the ends of her hair.

Tss-ss-ss-ss-ss-ss-ss...

Valerie held as still as humanly possible. The snake with the olive, leathery hide stared back, holding still, too. Diamond-shaped blotches along its back peppered into parallel stripes on its neck and head. Its black tongue flickered in and out, tasting the air. Psalm 121:7 ran over and over through Valerie's mind. *The Lord will protect you from all dangers; he will guard your life...The Lord will protect you from all dangers; he will guard your life....*

A drop of mud rolled casually down her forehead and between her eyes. Then it slid down her nose and stopped on the end, rocking side-to-side. Valerie's nose itched and her eyes began to water.

Then she heard another sound. A squeaking between her feet. *Oh, God, don't let that be a rat.* It was all she could do to keep from moving, from screaming, from crying.

In slow motion, the drop of mud cascaded off Valerie's nose. Valerie flinched. Without warning, the poisonous snake struck forward toward Valerie with its mouth open wide. Valerie leaped backward, trying to avoid the strike. As she hit the ground with the seat of her pants first, a splash of mud temporarily blocked her view. When it cleared, she saw the snake—all 4 feet of it, coiled up again, satisfied—with the tail of a small mouse dangling from its mouth. This was her opportunity.

Valerie kicked herself up with a sudden shot of adrenaline and splashed the mud hard, covering the snake. She took off running, first in the opposite direction, then in any direction with the least resistance. When she finally stopped to take a breath, she felt a cold chill of relief that she was finally alone.

She looked around her and took in the sight. Trees and leaves and vines and greenery were on every side. She had no idea where she was.

"Rapper!" she cried. "Rapper!"

No answer came.

She took a step forward...and before her eyes, the entire jungle shot quickly upward, leaving her in the dark.

It didn't take long for Valerie to realize what had happened. She had stepped into a trap. Literally. Lying on the ground in front of her had been an animal trap, concealed in greenery. And she had walked right into it. The hole she was standing in was about 6 feet deep and 4 feet in diameter. She barely fit, but that was actually the good news. It didn't look like it would be too hard to pull herself out.

She looked up and saw a primitively hinged door above her. It had snapped closed again after she fell through. First, she would have to open it, and then hold it open as she crawled out. Briefly, she wondered if Rapper had any idea that she was missing.

Valerie placed her hands on the muddy walls of the hole and pushed herself up. The mud oozed between her fingers and she made a promise to herself to always carry an extra pair of gloves. She raised herself up about 6 inches and stuck her shoes into the wall to fortify her position.

She reached up, but couldn't quite reach the trapdoor. Silently, she thanked God that when she fell in the hole, there was no animal inside it. That would have been all she needed—to be trapped in a 4-foot wide hole with a scared, untamed animal.

Suddenly, Valerie heard scratching on the ground above her. It was getting closer. A shadow covered the holes in the trapdoor above. The animal snorted. Valerie recognized the sound. It was a wild boar. A hog-like animal with a snout and short tail, a wild boar had two short, sharp horns stemming from either side of its jaw. Valerie had always been taught to stay far away from the heavy and squatty animals. Untamed and feisty, they'd been known to charge anyone who intruded their space. Valerie's eyes grew wide as she pictured it stepping on the trapdoor and dropping in on top of her. She raised one hand up toward the door as she used the other to balance herself on the side walls.

The wild boar was close—no doubt smelling Valerie's presence nearby. It would only be another moment before it realized she was beneath—

The trapdoor swung down as the boar stepped onto it with all of its weight. Valerie screamed as the door pressed down on her hand. She caught the door before it fell in far enough to throw the animal on top of her. The boar squealed and shrieked and scratched, surprised at its sudden dilemma.

Struggling to keep from being knocked from her footing in the muddy wall, Valerie thrust all her strength back at the trapdoor. She had to keep the boar out of the trap. In the back of her mind, she thanked God it was only a tiny boar—most likely a newborn. An adult could grow to weigh more than 200 pounds...and that could have literally crushed Valerie inside the hole.

The small, fat, gray-brown boar screamed and struggled, yearning to get free from the trap. Valerie pushed and pushed, but felt her left foot beginning to slip. Suddenly, the little boar got its footing and jumped free. The door shot back upward, but not before Valerie was able to grab hold of the corner. She let out a long sigh of relief as she heard the boar scampering away.

The young adventurer grabbed tightly onto the door's edge and worked to pull herself up. She pulled her feet out of the muddy walls and inched up slowly. She was pulling on the trap's door now with all her weight, forcing it to lie fully against the side of the muddy wall. As she raised her head above, the fading sunlight hit her eyes and she winced. Holding onto the door with her fingers, Valerie pushed off the muddy sides and kicked the air with short bursts. Her arms ached, but her body worked its way up out of the ground. Valerie flopped out of the hole onto her stomach. The trapdoor slammed shut on her right foot.

"Oww!" Valerie shouted and kicked the door with her other foot. It swung down for a moment, freeing her foot, but not before stealing her shoe. She took a few moments to catch her breath and then pushed the door open to look for the dirty, once-white cross trainer. It was all the way down at the bottom, lying upside down.

Valerie shook her head. It wasn't worth it. She'd find Rapper or her parents' village soon and everything would be all right.

She stood up, aching and asking God why her vacation had started out like this. A couple of hours had passed since she'd last seen Rapper and the sun was beginning to take its rest for the night. She couldn't see it directly from where she stood beneath the towering jungle above, but there was no doubt that it was getting darker. Shadows played all around her and nocturnal creatures were beginning to sound their claim on the territories surrounding them.

Valerie didn't want to be in the jungle when it got dark. To be honest, she wasn't sure why, but she always was told to stay away from the jungle at night. And she had always obeyed.

A twig snapped. Valerie jumped. Nothing happened.

Valerie closed her eyes and took a deep breath. "I will be strong and brave. I won't be afraid, Lord, because I know Your Word says in Joshua 1:9 that You are with me everywhere I go."

A distant animal shrieked. Valerie shrieked too. She was trying hard to be brave, to not fear—just like God's Word said—but the darkness was creeping in and the wild animals were calling to one another. It was just plain unsettling.

"Psalm 91. I'll say Psalm 91 to myself. That will help me to not be afraid."

As Valerie walked through the jungle, carefully watching for more traps, tropical rattlesnakes, wild boars and other snares, she began to pray the Word she had memorized years ago.

"As I go to God Most High for safety I will be protected by God All-Powerful. I will say to the LORD, 'You are my place of safety and protection. You are my God, and I trust You.' God will save me from hidden traps..." Valerie thought about what she was saying and felt strength come to her. "...and from deadly diseases. He will protect me like a bird spreading its wings over its young. His truth will be like my armor and shield. I will not fear any danger by night or an arrow during the day." Valerie looked around her at the darkening underbrush. She gulped. "I will not be afraid of diseases that come in the dark or sickness that strikes at noon. I will not be hurt. I will only watch what happens. I will see the wicked punished. The Lord is my protection. I have made God Most High my place of safety. Nothing bad will happen to me. No disaster will come to my home. He has put His angels in charge of me." The thought of big, strong angels at her side comforted her again. "They will watch over me wherever I go. They will catch me with their hands. And I will not hit my foot on a rock. I will walk on lions and cobras. I will step on strong lions and snakes." Valerie stopped and looked at the ground, thanking God it wasn't moving. She wiggled her sock-covered toes on the foot missing a shoe. She began stepping forward again. "The LORD says, 'If someone loves me, I will save him. I will protect those who know me. They will call to me, and I will answer them. I will be with them in trouble. I will rescue them and honor them. I will give them a long, full life. They will see how I can save.'"

A light, nightfall breeze cooled the tiny scrapes she had on her face and bare arms from running through the jungle earlier. Valerie stopped walking and listened to the quiet, darkened evening around her. She realized it was probably lighter away from the jungle, but deep inside, the leaves of the tall trees blocked any remaining sunlight.

On her left, Valerie could hear insects chirping and leaves brushing against each other. On her right, she heard something slithering over the drying underbrush of the jungle floor. Above her, a bird flew into its nest. Though she felt strength from speaking God's Word aloud, the jungle still felt creepy. And for all she knew, she was walking in circles.

Tss-ss-ss-ss-ss-ss-ss...

Valerie froze and held her breath. *Not another rattler!* she thought. She slowly looked all around her...but in the dark it was difficult to tell a vine from an olive-colored rattlesnake.

Tss-ss-ss-ss-ss-ss-ss...

Then Valerie realized the sound was coming from *above* her. *Way* above her. *The SuperCopter!*

"Rapper!"

Looking up, Valerie couldn't see anything but towering trees and a lightning bug dancing here or there. She figured Rapper couldn't see down to her any easier. Valerie had to find a way to signal him...but she had nothing at her disposal to use. No flare, no flag, not even a whistle. The sound faded. She leaned back on the nearest tree trunk and huffed. She was in trouble. She was hungry. She was thirsty. She was lost.

Tss-ss-ss-ss-ss-ss-ss...

There it was again! Hope rose in Valerie's tender heart and she knew she had to at least try *something*. Turning around, she grabbed onto the nearest fuzzy tree trunk. Using a technique she'd learned in one of Superkid Academy's field training classes, Valerie began scaling the thick tree. She pulled with her hands and pushed with her feet, forcing her reluctant body up the towering tree.

The first branches were nearly halfway up. When Valerie reached them, she grabbed onto the sturdiest looking one and looked down. Her head swam as she saw how high she'd come. On the ground below, the twigs and leaves looked like needles and pebbles. She looked back up and stopped the dizziness by momentarily closing her eyes. She had a ways to go. She listened for the SuperCopter, but didn't hear it any longer. Still, Rapper might return...she hoped.

She climbed up higher still, reaching from one branch to another. That's when it happened. A weak branch snapped under her grasp, throwing the Superkid off balance. She screamed as she dropped about 10 feet, then stopped herself by grabbing onto the first branch she found. Her hands burned as she hung in the open air, dangling from the bending limb. She pulled up, trying to get on top of the thin branch, or at least closer to another one...but the more she exerted herself, the more the limb bent.

Snap!

That was it. No warning. The branch broke in two, dropping Valerie down farther. She yelped. She looked up to see that she was still hanging—but only by a couple of fibers in the branch. Surely, soon they would also—

Rrrip!

Valerie went sailing down the remaining length of the tree, heading straight for the packed ground below. When she hit, she suddenly swallowed her scream, surprised that she didn't feel much. It was as if she had been caught.

Of course, that was because she *was* caught. By someone with the darkest skin she'd ever seen. And the darkest eyes.

Frightened by the unexpected, she screamed again.

Her rescuer screamed back.

And then Valerie fainted.

When Valerie began to stir, the first thing she sensed was the sweet smell of herbs and spices wafting through the air. Her back felt warm and she could hear the crackling of a fire behind her. As her eyelids opened, she saw the darkened jungle forest in front of her. The soft sounds of critters singing and wild animals hooting brought back memories of the sweet, summer nights she used to spend lying in her bed in her family's island hut. Made of jungle materials and thick clay, the hut housed separate rooms for her and her parents while offering a living room (of sorts) next to a small kitchen and indoor bathroom. The bathroom, of course, was the epitome of luxury in her Calypso Island home.

She used to lie in her bed and listen to the jungle come alive at night. The relaxing sounds triggered her imagination and she dreamed of one day being a missionary herself—just like her mom and dad. As she grew older, her dream changed, but her desire for ministry remained as she began to picture herself instead as a commander at Superkid Academy...not unlike her mentor, Commander Kellie.

Valerie worked hard every day to show herself willing and able to meet the toughest of assignments.

From piloting tests and academics to physically challenging Academy courses, Valerie almost always came out on top. And most importantly, she would spend much of her free time digging deep into God's Word. Reading it, studying it, praying about it—she did anything to grow stronger in Him. She knew that's what it took to be a commander. And one day, as far as Valerie was concerned, she *would* be one.

Valerie yawned, stretching her arms and legs. When her yawn pushed into her toes, a chill crawled up her spine as she realized her feet were covered only with socks. Quickly, it all rushed back to her—the encounter with the snake, getting lost in the jungle, falling into the trap, climbing the tree, dropping from the tree, landing in the arms of—

Valerie sat up fast and whirled herself around. Her head pounded as the vision of a small bonfire filled her eyes. Momentarily she imagined that the fire was heating up to cook someone's dinner...and she was going to be the main course! But the thought disintegrated with the little silver stars that danced like snowflakes before her eyes.

Inside the miniature clearing, the fire burned hot, surrounded by stones. On either side of it, a couple thick sticks shaped like 'Y's held a spear directly over the fire, creating an 'H' shape. A crude pan set in the middle of the fire had speckles of the herbs and spices Valerie smelled inside it. Valerie looked around, but didn't see anyone near. Apparently, whoever had gone to all the trouble to make dinner hadn't returned with it yet.

Valerie pressed on the back of her neck, attempting to alleviate the intrusion of a light headache. Her stomach growled as she took in the fresh herbal scent, now stronger than just a few minutes before. She stood up, stretched again and looked down at her body. It was the first time she had taken a moment to notice she was covered with mud from head to toe—dried now, which made it even more disgusting to her. Her tank top, originally olive green, now had a camouflage look with swirls of brown and green. Her jeans were stiff from the dried, caked mud. Valerie tugged at each of her socks, but they were just as stiff. She looked at her watch, but it wasn't working any longer. Normally, she would have been wearing a more durable communications watch, or "ComWatch" as they were called, but since she had gone on vacation, she didn't think she would need the high-tech item. Next time, Valerie convinced herself, *that* would be the *first* thing she'd pack. Not only would she know the time, but she would also be able to communicate with others via the lightweight viewing screen. *Next time,* Valerie thought again. *Next time.*

Snap! Snap!

Valerie's eyes grew wide. The hair on the back of her neck stood up on end, like falling dominoes in reverse.

There it was. Across the small campsite, on the opposite side of the fire, a small human figure froze in its tracks. It was too dark to see, but Valerie could make out a few lighter marks on its face...some kind of tribal markings most likely.

Valerie squinted hard and it looked like the figure was squinting back. It was holding some long pieces of rope or vine—Valerie wasn't sure which. Her first inclination was to run with all her might, far, far away from the unsurety and uncertainty of the situation. A loud gulp suppressed a scream she wanted to let out. Valerie could feel the heat of fear warming up her hands and face.

Be strong, be brave...

Knowing there was nowhere she could run, Valerie began to inch toward the figure.

"H-hello," she stammered. She took a few more steps. The figure didn't move, but took in her every action.

"I-I-I, uh, wanted to thank you for saving my, uh, life." As she passed by the side of the burning logs, drawing closer, the light enabled her to see him better. He was a tall boy with dark skin and without a shirt. He had a gray cloth tied around the lower portion of his body. Around his left hand and hiding his thumb, he wore a thick band of white cloth marked with a black skull. On his chest and face, he wore the painted white markings of a tribe, as Valerie had guessed.

Valerie kept progressing toward the stranger—carefully—praying he wouldn't find anything she did offensive.

"Wh-What's your name?" she asked, not really expecting an answer. She was in front of the young stranger now, staring him in the eyes. He didn't blink or change his facial expression.

"I-I'm trying to find m-m-m-mmmm..." Valerie stopped and calmed herself, pressing at the air around her with open palms. She huffed, releasing the stress. "I'm trying to find my friend and my way back home."

"Yrgnuh m'i!" the native cried. Valerie shook at the sudden outburst. Her heart raced faster and it was all she could do to keep from taking off running.

"I-I don't understand," Valerie whimpered back. "I really mean no harm. I'm just a bit frightened. It's dark and creepy and you surprised me. I'm sorry. I really mean you no harm." Valerie cupped her mouth with her hands. She was beginning to sound like Missy, her roommate back at Superkid Academy. Whenever Missy wasn't sure what to say, she'd begin to ramble. And Valerie felt like she was doing just that.

Suddenly, off to the side and high up in a tree a monkey screamed. Valerie jumped and screamed herself. The native laughed, exposing shiny, yellow teeth.

"What?!" Valerie wondered out loud.

"Hee-hee-hee! Yeknom a tsuj s'ti!" the native replied, still chuckling. Now he was pointing at Valerie.

"What?!" Valerie insisted, not sure what to make of the native's humor at her expense. The native boy covered his mouth.

"You have to understand *some* language," Valerie reasoned. "How about '¡Hola! ¿Cómo estás?'" she said, trying out her Spanish. He didn't move.

"Bonsoir," she said, making French her next choice. Nothing.

"Ellohay!" No response. Pig Latin wasn't his thing, either.

"Girl funny," he finally said.

"You *do* speak English!" Valerie shouted, amazed.

"Only little," the boy replied. "Girl funny. Girl scared."

Valerie's heart began to slow down again. "Well, I don't think it's funny."

"I do, hee-hee-hee." The young native laughed. Then Valerie laughed.

"I guess I am a *little* jumpy."

"Girl grasshopper."

"I'm not a *grasshopper.*"

"Girl little grasshopper. Girl green, brown, and hop, hop, hop." Valerie looked at her outfit again. It was all green and brown, like a grasshopper.

"Well, I don't 'hop, hop, hop.'"

"Girl hop, hop, hop. Here, there. Up tree, down tree." The boy walked past Valerie and headed across the campsite. As he walked by, the scent of fresh-cut grass followed. Valerie noticed for the first time that his ears were pierced and each one held a wooden ornament. "Hop, hop, hop," he taunted as he walked away. "Hee-hee-hee."

A sudden realization hit Valerie head on. "Wait!" she shouted. "Don't go! I need your help!"

"Time for food. We talk later."

"No. We need to talk now. My parents are nearby, but I don't know where. If you can just tell me the direction, I'll go—"

"Girl go in jungle alone? No. Girl too scared."

"I am not scared. I don't have any fear." Another monkey chirped. Valerie jumped. The young native laughed. Valerie crossed her arms in defense.

"No, girl no fear. Hee-hee-hee. Girl funny. Girl stay here."

Valerie looked around her at the dancing shadows created by the hot fire.

"Oh, no. I'm coming with *you.*"

The boy raised his eyebrows, wrinkling his dark forehead.

"You may need my help," Valerie explained.

"Help? From—" He pointed at Valerie and shook his head. "Hee-hee-hee." He began to walk. Despite what he said, Valerie followed. She noticed that even though he was barefoot, his steps were very deliberate. Valerie, on the other hand, tried to judge her every step, even though she had the protection of stiff socks. When possible, she stepped in the very prints her new friend imprinted in the grassy field.

"You don't happen to know what happened to my one shoe, do you?" Valerie inquired. The native boy looked over his shoulder as he walked.

"How girl think fire start?"

"Oh, great."

"Hee-hee-hee."

A few more steps and the two adventurers stopped. The boy fiddled with the vine he was carrying and made a hoop out of one end. It was a lot longer than Valerie had thought and she couldn't imagine what it was he was doing. He kept working and Valerie noticed he let his left thumb remain hidden under the cloth.

"So how old are you?" she asked, oblivious to his work. He held up his nine visible fingers.

"You're 9?" He held up four more and then continued to tie the vine. "Plus 4. You're 13. I'm about that old, too. I'll have my 13th birthday not too long from now. Well, actually, it's a couple years, but who's counting?"

The boy threw half the vine straight up. It curled around the thick branch of a tall tree and sailed back down. He caught it and placed the hoop on the ground. He gathered some sticks and rocks and began to place them in precise spots, meticulously tying some to the free end.

"So what's your name?" Valerie asked.

"Cayseilauphlan."

"Huh?"

"Means 'Cunning One.' Cayseilauphlan learn fast. Cayseilauphlan learn English fast from leader. *And* Cayseilauphlan learn to make trap in only one week."

With that, the boy began to tie what looked like tiny bows in the vine. As he did, the tree branch above began to bend further and further. The vine was quickly taut.

"How about if I call you 'Casey?' My name's Valerie. You can call me 'Val.'"

"Okey-dokey. Hallo, Val."

Valerie giggled. "Okey-dokey. Hello, Casey."

Casey snapped his head up, like a radar catching an unknown signal. "Come, Val. We go," he whispered. Quickly, the two young people moved back into the camp and walked toward the fire.

For the first time, Valerie felt relaxed enough to take in all of Casey's features. His hair was curly, dark black and very short. His bare skin was a chocolate brown and speckled with distinct, white tribal markings. None of them looked familiar to Valerie. She had met a lot of tribes and people during her life on Calypso Island, but—strangely enough—Casey's tribal marks weren't like any she'd seen.

Casey sat down on the log Valerie had been napping on earlier. She took a seat beside him. He stared into the fire. Somehow, Valerie felt completely comfortable with Casey now. She'd always found it easy to make new friends, plus just knowing she wasn't alone in the dark was comforting. Still, every once in a while, a twig would snap or a monkey would scream and Valerie would jump, frightened by the sudden sound in the night.

"How long have you been on Calypso Island," she gently asked. Casey's forehead wrinkled.

"We no on Calypso. We on Jungle Island."

Valerie's stomach tightened. "W-w-w-we're on *Jungle* Island?!"

"Val lost," he replied. And he was right. Valerie knew Jungle Island was about two miles southwest of Calypso. It was a dense island, comprised mostly of jungle, and inhabited by not only a variety of wild animals, but also a ruthless tribe of natives called the Manwans. Rumors and vicious tales spread about their tribal practices. They'd always threatened the lives of intruders and many intruders never returned.

As the fire flashed and reality set in, Valerie first began to worry about Rapper, but then figured he was all right since she'd heard him take off. Then she began to worry about herself. What if she ran into one of the Manwans? She looked at Casey's hand and eyed the cloth marked with the skull. Then again, maybe she already had.

Five hours passed and neither Valerie nor Casey said much of anything. Both their stomachs growled with hunger and every once in a while Casey would get up and check out the trap he had set, but nothing notable happened. At one point, Casey brought Valerie a small bowl of water so she could wash herself. She splashed the water on her face and arms in an attempt to drive the dirt away. Most of her face was clear now, but her hair, clothes and upper arms still told the tale of her adventure.

Fear had kept Valerie quite awake and worry had made her queasy. She felt like she could trust Casey—her spirit felt comfortable with him. But her mind continually prodded her to run...escape into the jungle... and had she not felt so weak from lack of nourishment, she just might have.

"I've got to get out of here," Valerie whispered. Her words caused Casey to stir.

"What Val say?"

"I said I've got to get out of here. It's getting lighter. If I just head east, toward the rising sun, I'll surely hit the beach sooner or later. Maybe Rapper will spot me..."

"Val cannot leave."

Valerie spun her head around, causing her hair to brush her cheeks. "What?!" Her eyes beamed at Casey. Was he threatening her?

"Too dangerous. If my people find Val, they no let Val live."

Valerie's head dropped in discouragement. "Your people...They're the Manwans, aren't they?"

Casey nodded. "Val know of Manwans. Manwans bad when they scared."

"What do you mean? What are *they* scared of? From what I've heard, most people are scared of *them.*"

"Manwan scared of people they no know. Manwan scared of things they no know."

"So because they don't know me, I may scare them and they may hurt me?"

Casey nodded. Valerie swallowed hard.

"But Casey," she inquired gently, "if you're Manwan, why didn't you hurt me?"

Casey pushed out his chest. "Because Cayseilauphlan no scared. Cayseilauphlan brave...no bad."

Valerie could feel her heart beating within her chest. "I believe you," she said softly, squeezing his bare arm. He kept looking straight ahead.

"Casey," Valerie pressed on, "maybe if you take me to your people, they will not be scared of me. And maybe they can help me find my way to Calypso Island. Maybe they can help me find my way home."

The rising sun shot thin beams of heat through the jungle brush. Valerie felt its soothing warmth on her arms.

"No."

"No?!"

"Cayseilauphlan no can. We must both stay away."

"So I'm your prisoner here? If I leave, I either get eaten by wild animals or captured by an even wilder tribe? Is that it?"

"We both prisoner."

"I don't understand, Casey."

"Cayseilauphlan no longer Manwan."

Valerie waited for an explanation, but none came. The morning dew chilled the air, the fire was only a spark and the spices had lost their aroma. Casey slid off the log and moved to put the fire out completely.

"Casey, you can't do this."

Casey turned around and faced Valerie. She could see the soft orange glow of daybreak reflecting in his eyes. He looked sad, like he'd lost his favorite puppy. He looked at her, questioning.

"You have to tell me what's going on. *Why* aren't you Manwan anymore? *Why* are you alone, out in the jungle all night long? *Why* are you going hungry?"

The native boy twisted his lips to the right, then again to the left. It was obvious to Valerie that he was holding something in. A secret. A deep secret that he was afraid for her to know. A dark secret that had driven him away from his family and from his people.

"Cayseilauphlan no longer Manwan because Cayseilauphlan scare Manwans."

Finally, Valerie thought, *some kind of explanation.* Now if she could only get him to speak in a way she could understand.

"So you scare your own people," she said more as a statement than a question.

"Cayseilauphlan scare Manwans because of this." Casey pointed to the cloth band with the black skull on it. "This Manwans no understand. This scare Manwans. They make Cayseilauphlan leave—no come back."

Valerie stared at the band. What was it that scared an entire tribe so bad that they would order a young boy to leave and never return? Valerie hopped off the log and stood in front of Casey. Dew droplets trickled off the grass blades, onto her socked feet, soaking the socks clear through. She reached forward slowly toward the band. Casey recoiled immediately.

"No! Val no touch!" Casey's face was wrinkled with fear, leaving Valerie speechless. With caution, she put her hands back at her sides. Casey relaxed and then reached over to the band himself. "Cayseilauphlan let Val see."

Casey carefully rolled the band back, but only about an inch...just enough for Valerie to see what was underneath it. His thumb and the round section of skin below it were no longer the beautiful, dark color that covered the rest of Casey's body. It was extremely light brown instead. It looked rough and fragile at the same time. And it was covered with a cluster of red knots.

Casey rolled the band back up and sat down on the log, defeated and ashamed. Valerie felt suspended in time for a moment, like if she moved she might shatter the world around her.

Her mind was dull from lack of sleep and food, but Valerie knew immediately what it was: H.D...Hansen's disease...better known as *leprosy*. Most people didn't even know the fatal, ancient disease was around anymore—but Casey obviously did. A vicious plague that attacks a person's skin and nerves, leprosy eventually affects a person's whole body—making them weak and fragile. And even worse, the disease is contagious when someone is exposed to it for a long time and with close contact. She remembered asking Commander Kellie about it once when they were studying Jesus' miracles in the Bible. The New Testament told about Him healing people with leprosy...people society had abandoned. People just like Casey. No wonder his tribe made him an outcast.

"Are there others?" Valerie asked.

"Many years ago," Casey responded. "Manwans thought disease was gone. Then disease found on me."

"So you're alone," Valerie whispered, staring at the skull on the band.

"Val no like Casey now?" the young man asked, using the nickname Valerie had given him. She could feel her heart break inside as compassion warmed her from head to toe. She knew Someone Whose power was greater than any disease of the devil—including leprosy.

"Oh, no, Casey. Your arm doesn't scare me—I'm not going to leave you. We're going to get through this. And I believe we'll each find our home again."

Fa-TWANNNGG! SQUEEEEE!

Valerie and Casey's words were interrupted by the sound and squeal of a wild boar stepping right into Casey's trap. The horned hog shot up into the air, caught by the legs and, to Valerie's surprise, despite its weight, it kept going up. The two young people ran toward the trap. They lost sight of the animal when it sailed high above the tree tops. At once, Valerie remembered the flying pig she and Rapper saw on their ride in; so they weren't mistaken after all!

"Oops," was all Casey offered to say as he watched and waited for the wild boar to come back down. Several seconds later, Valerie saw its brown tail come into view, followed by its hindquarters, belly and finally its head.

"*...eeeeeeEEEEEEE!!!!!!*" The boar came back down and stopped shy of the ground by about 3 feet. It bounced up and down in the air, squealing and snorting.

"You caught a wild boar!" Valerie applauded. Casey was all smiles.

"Vine a little tight—still learning," he explained. Valerie shook her head. During her early years, she had wild boar many times for supper—her mother would cook it. And now her stomach was growling even more.

▲   ▲   ▲

"This is wonderful!" Valerie complimented as she took another bite of the spiced, wild pork that Chef Casey had cooked. It was hot, juicy and extremely tasty. Maybe it was because she was so hungry, but Valerie couldn't remember the last time she'd had such a fulfilling meal.

The boar they'd caught was really pretty small, but for two young people, it was more than enough for a couple days. Valerie wiped her mouth with a large leaf Casey provided for their dining pleasure. She tried to cut and eat her pork steak with sticks earlier, but it was more difficult than handy, so now, like Casey, she resorted to finishing her meal with her hands. Of course, Casey had several knives and small tools that he used to prepare the meal, but they were all too awkward and overbearing to use as dining utensils.

Valerie chuckled as she imagined her best friend, Missy Ashton, in a situation like this. *She'd be throwing a fit,* Valerie thought. Valerie would describe Missy as the type who doesn't find huge enjoyment in "extreme nature-and-earth" situations. Missy planned to join Valerie and Rapper on their trip to Calypso, but she pulled away at the last minute when Paul, another Superkid, decided to go to the city of Nautical for his vacation. Since Nautical was Missy's hometown, she couldn't pass up the opportunity. Valerie really wanted her to come to Calypso, but given the present situation she deemed it better that Missy hadn't come. *I'm sure she's having a nice, normal, relaxing time at her own home,* Valerie imagined. *Meanwhile I'm in the middle of an unexplored island surrounded by ferocious animals and hostile natives. Boy, will we have stories to swap.*

Valerie finished her meal and sat back in the grass, against the familiar log. A knob in the wood hit her in the small of her back and she scooted over a few inches. She watched Casey finish his meal and her heart went out to him. Here was a boy who wouldn't even get to become a man if the leprosy were allowed to continue spreading. The way Valerie saw it, Satan was robbing him of his life. He was trying to steal her new friend's last breaths. Valerie had attended Superkid Academy and read God's Word long enough to know that this just wasn't right. Casey's destiny wasn't an early death. According to God's Word in Psalm 91:16, his destiny should be a long, full life. *That* was God's will. Now she just had to convince Casey of that.

"Casey," Valerie interrupted his feasting to ask him an important question, "do you know you can be healed from your disease?"

Casey looked up from his pork. "Hmm?"

"You can be healed," Valerie continued. "God is the answer."

"Cayseilauphlan ask god to heal him. No do."

"You've asked God? W-wait a second," she stammered. "What god?" She ran her fingers through her bobbed, brown hair. It was matted in clumps and granules of dirt shook free. She couldn't wait for a decent bath and shampoo.

"Cayseilauphlan ask Manwan god—Guphigai."

Valerie laughed out loud for the first time since she and Rapper landed on Jungle Island the day before. *"Goofyguy?!* Your god's name is 'Goofyguy?!'"

Casey simply blinked. He didn't see the humor. Valerie grabbed his hand.

"Casey, look. You've said you asked your god for healing. Nothing happened. I challenge you to ask mine. The God I serve is the God above all gods—even your Goofyguy god."

"Val's God heal Cayseilauphlan?"

"I know He can. He can take away your fear, Casey. He can make you completely well."

"If Val's God take away Cayseilauphlan's fear of sickness, why Val's God no take away Val's fear of jungle?"

Valerie's mouth went dry and she felt like she'd just been slugged in the stomach. Here she was telling him that God would free him from sickness and the fear of it...yet ever since they had met, Valerie had lived in fear of the jungle. She feared the animals. She feared the natives. She even feared Casey when they first met. She was acting just like the Manwans. She was fearing the unknown.

"You're right," she whispered as the realization hit her. "Here I've been confessing and praying against fear. I've been trying to apply God's principles of faith in my life...but...I've never faced my underlying fear of being alone—and the devil has robbed me every step of the way."

Without another word, Valerie made a decision—a promise to herself—that she would not operate in fear any longer. Instead, she would exercise her faith, even in the jungle. It wouldn't be easy...and surely the tests would come. But she wanted to defeat it once and for all. *God, give me wisdom,* she thought.

Valerie proceeded to share the gospel with Casey. She told him about how much God loved him. How He sent His only Son, Jesus, to die for each person alive—including Casey. And when Jesus died and rose again He not only took away Casey's sin, but He also took away his disease and his fears.

Casey listened intently and nodded. When she asked him if he wanted to make Jesus his Lord, Casey answered by saying, "Cayseilauphlan want to see Val's God take Val's fear."

Valerie understood. The young man wanted to see that God was real—and he wanted to see it in Valerie first. She was God's reflection to Casey. Then she knew, more than ever, that she needed to get entirely free of her fear. Because if she didn't, Casey might be led to believe his god was mightier than hers. And Val wasn't about to let some Goofyguy show her God up. She set her jaw and fixed her eyes upon Casey's.

"You'll see," she promised. "My God is the God above all gods. He will come through for us." Casey nodded.

Valerie grabbed his hand. "Let me pray for you," she stated, rather than asking permission. She couldn't help it. Anyone would agree that the Word was so deep inside Valerie that when she saw someone sick or hurting, she couldn't help but speak up and pray. She once told Missy that it was like "a fire" in her hands. If she didn't just pray for someone right away, her fingertips would be filled with heat until she did. Missy was just being honest when she said she thought that was a little "different"...but she didn't doubt what Valerie was saying was true.

Valerie placed her hands on top of Casey's head and began to pray.

"Father God, I come before You in the Name of Jesus. I lift my new friend Casey up to You. God, You know all about this disease that has attacked him. But it doesn't scare You. So, I thank You first of all that Jesus took away this disease 2,000 years ago when He died for Casey. And today, I set my faith for Casey's complete healing. But I pray that his first healing is spiritual. May he come to know You as his Lord and Savior. And I pray that his mind is also healed. Your Word says in 1 Corinthians 2:16 that we have the mind of Christ. And I pray today that his thoughts agree with

Your Word. And finally I pray for healing of his body. May it be an example of what has happened in the other areas of his life. By Your wounds, Casey has been healed. That's what 1 Peter 2:24 says. We will believe it today. And Holy Spirit, lead us home. In Jesus' Name, amen!"

Valerie looked up and Casey's eyes were wide. Valerie thought at first that she had just prayed too long for him. But once she started talking to God, it was hard for her to stop.

"Cayseilauphlan feel heat," the boy whispered.

"What do you mean?"

"Val's hands give heat to Cayseilauphlan," he explained.

"That's the power of God flowing from me to you. It doesn't always happen that way, but He's showing Himself to you, Casey. He wants you to receive your healing." Casey nodded again.

Tss-ss-ss-ss-ss-ss-ss!

Valerie jumped up and searched the area around her, looking for the threatening rattler. At this point, she felt charged enough to take on just about anything—including the meanest snake alive. But then she realized that once again it wasn't a snake she heard—it was the SuperCopter!

Valerie hopped up and eyed the sky for a glimpse of her friend, but soon the whir of the chopper's blades faded away and they were alone once more. Valerie huffed.

"He hasn't given up," she said to herself. Then she turned to Casey. "Friend," she began, "we have to find a way to Calypso Island. The jungle is too thick for

Rapper to find us. If you'll come with me, you can stay with us. Until you receive your healing, my father surely has some medicine that can help you. Will you do it? Will you help me?"

Casey looked at her blankly and then smiled.

"Cayseilauphlan have plan."

Casey's plan was slightly less planned than Valerie had hoped, but it was their best option yet. He explained their next move as he led her through the thick brush of the jungle. He angled left, then right, then left again as they traveled through the leafy maze. Valerie was glad Casey was with her. Finding her way out alone would have been difficult, not to mention dangerous.

Every once in a while, Valerie would hear something that sounded threatening, but her guide never stopped. He simply steered in another direction, avoiding entrapment altogether.

"Val no fear," he stated as they sneaked around. "Animals no attack Val, unless Val attack animals." Casey went on to explain to Valerie that most of the jungle animals would never attack a human just for the sake of attacking. Most would only fight if they were attacked first—or if they were extremely hungry. Even the wild boars, which had a reputation for being notably feisty, only charged humans if they got too close. Casey explained to Valerie how boars simply like to keep a safe distance from others—and if you're wise, you'll keep a safe distance from them. Between their sharp horns and their quick, hoofed feet, a person wouldn't want to be in the wrong place at the wrong time. That's why Casey used a vine sling to capture the wild boar for dinner. It was far safer than throwing a spear at the animal...for if he missed, he might have been the one speared!

At the edge of the jungle Casey finally stopped and Valerie was thankful for a moment to catch her breath. As she breathed in the warm air, she looked down at her feet and smiled. On her left foot she wore her cross-training shoe—Casey had only been joking about using it to start the fire. It was nearly as dirty as the sock she wore inside it, but it didn't seem to matter much now. Most importantly, Valerie just wanted to get off the dangerous island—clean or not.

On her right foot, she wore a makeshift shoe Casey put together for her. He thought she'd move faster on the unfamiliar ground with two shoes. The shoe sole was simply 10 strong leaves stuck together with some type of sap. He bound it around her foot with a vine. Casey didn't want shoes for himself, though. He showed her how the bottoms of his feet had hardened to the ground, making it easier for him. He wasn't nearly as concerned about thorns or sticks or even angry, little bugs.

Casey pointed through some brush toward the beach beyond. Then he pointed left to a large structure blocking anyone from continuing down the beach. The structure looked like a huge, solid box of logs. Long, light-brown tree trunks lay parallel, sealed atop one another with thick, solidified, homemade glue. There was a solitary window, cut out on the side. On the far right, a series of logs glued together stood on end and created a hefty door. Valerie noted the interesting hinges that allowed it to swing open and closed. Then she thanked God that it was closed. The roof of the building was created by more of the rolling trunks covering the top at a sharp angle. All together, the crude, log warehouse appeared foreboding and secretive. Extending out from both sides of the building was a tall, tree-trunk fence. The Manwans didn't want anyone to know an entire boat yard was on the other side.

"Cayseilauphlan boat over there," Casey promised, pointing to the building. The plan was simple—or so it seemed. All they had to do was get into the boat yard, on the other side of the building, grab the boat that belonged to Casey and row home to Calypso.

"Sounds *too* easy," Valerie offered. That's when Casey went on to explain that there were two guards inside the log building and that the boat yard was filled with nearly 100 boats—half of which were unfinished. If they grabbed any other boat than the one he created with his own two hands, they may not get very far.

"Val know plan?" Casey asked with his dark eyebrows raised. Valerie nodded.

"Val know plan. I just hope it works."

Casey smiled a toothy smile. "Cayseilauphlan plan always work."

Valerie smirked and grabbed the right hand of her new friend. "Thank you for everything, Casey. I believe that my God will bring us through."

Casey began to push forward, but then stopped and turned momentarily. "Val no fear?"

Valerie blinked noticeably and let out a long, deep breath. "I won't," she replied. Casey smiled again and went his way to fulfill his part of the plan. But the truth was, Valerie was terrified. The more she thought about the fact that at any moment she could be running from merciless natives, the more her knees began to knock...and the more her heart began to race...and the more her chin quivered. But she was going to make it through—she had made a decision to face the fear by trusting in God's Word. She wasn't just thinking about herself anymore. Now she was considering Casey, too. Both their lives were on the line.

▲　▲　▲

Casey had been gone for nearly five minutes and Valerie knew it was time to make her move. Her job, according to the young native's plan, was to just get into the boat yard without being seen. Once there, Casey would catch up, they'd find his boat and they'd be off. It seemed simple enough. Casey's part of the plan was to get rid of the guards—a job he was sure he could handle.

Valerie walked near the edge of the jungle as she secretly made her way toward the boat yard, avoiding the open window at all costs. She hadn't actually seen the boat yard itself yet, so she wasn't sure what to expect. As she stayed at the jungle edge and neared the wooden structure blocking her route, she heard a sound.

"Pssst!"

It was Casey. He was standing by the looming front door. He made an upward motion with his hand and Valerie looked at the dense path ahead of her. The tall, camouflaged, wooden fence was much too high to climb and too far to go around. Her only option was to go through the building...or over it. And going through was not her first choice.

The Superkid nodded. *I will be strong and brave, Lord, because I know You are with me everywhere I go,* she whispered Joshua 1:9 to herself.

Carefully, Valerie tiptoed out of the jungle. She crossed to the front of the building and peered at the logs. *This shouldn't be too hard to climb,* she reasoned. She had climbed much higher and smoother structures in her Superkid Academy physical training program. First, she placed her "leaf shoe" on the second row of trunks making up the structure. Then, once she had a secure hold, Valerie pushed off the ground with her other foot, jumping up, and grabbed on as high as she could with her hands. She continued her climb, one hand and foot in front of the other. She successfully scaled halfway up the wall before...

Thump.

Valerie's good shoe missed its foothold and hit hard on the side of the wall. Valerie gasped, but swallowed her voice, not wanting to alert anyone to her presence. But it was too late. Through the open window below her, she could hear a couple of men's voices speaking loudly in another language.

Down below, Casey deliberately shouted at the door. The two voices silenced temporarily—*like the calm before a storm,* Valerie thought.

Seconds later, the door swung open and the two men emerged. Valerie was holding on for dear life, tightening her grip as the seconds passed. Her arm muscles tightened and she saw her arms turn red as her blood zipped through them. The stark contrast of her reddish skin against her olive and brown, mud-caked tank top was almost comical. But Valerie wasn't in the mood to laugh.

The men were easy to identify as Manwans, since the white markings on their faces and bare chests were similar to Casey's. One had no hair at all, and the other had long, woven braids. Both men were in their late 20s, Valerie guessed. Like Casey, they were barefoot and wore a gray cloths tied around their waists for clothing.

"T'naw ooy od tahw!" the bald one yelled. Casey didn't lose his composure. He had a whole clump of vines draped over his left shoulder. He hid his telltale handband behind them. He pulled one vine out of the bunch with his right hand and held it up to the natives.

"Elas rof! Eno t'naw?" he shouted. The two natives' foreheads wrinkled. Valerie knew it was her opportunity. Casey was distracting the two guards— distracting them so she could get to the other side. Valerie slowly pushed herself up as quietly as she could. She didn't want to attract any attention by sudden movement. As she climbed, the two men conversed with Casey and the one with the braided hair began to yell at Casey, pointing sharply in his face. He was moving his head back and forth as he complained about something. To Valerie, his complaining sounded a lot like whining. *Sounds the same in every language,* she thought.

Finally, her fingers reached the log rooftop and Valerie pulled herself up. She looked down, but then pulled her eyes away. She was higher than she thought. She didn't like this already. She would rather leave the climbing and fighting adventures to Rapper. Since he was once part of a street gang, he was a bit more fit for the whole "adventure lifestyle." True, he hadn't been on the street for more than four years now—ever since he discovered that true power is in Jesus and not weapons—but that didn't mean he didn't still have the "street smarts" in him when situations like this arose.

But you have the wisdom and mind of Christ, the Holy Spirit spoke to Valerie, reminding her of Proverbs 4:1 and 1 Corinthians 2:16. Valerie brought her thoughts into line with the Word. He was right. She could make it through this with His help.

Squatting down, Valerie scooted awkwardly up the sharply angled roof and reached the top in no time. She tried to peer over into the boat yard, but with the large leaves and branches of nearby trees blocking her way, she couldn't see much. The natives' voices were muffled now, and by their tone it sounded like they were tired of bartering and were trying to get Casey to go away. She didn't have much time.

Valerie hopped over the hump and steadied herself to carefully head down the other side...but when her leaf-shoe came down on the first log making up the roof's sharp angle, she lost her footing. Valerie slipped down onto the rooftop, barely blocking a blow to the back of her head. Lying flat on her back, she flipped over, frantically trying to get a handhold on the angled top of the roof. But the force of gravity coupled with the slickness left from the recent rain made it difficult to grab. In moments, she was cascading down the roof, feet first, sliding and gasping for quick breaths.

When she reached the edge, her feet were the first to fly over, followed by her knees. As she slid without any control, her tank top pulled up a few inches, burning her stomach against the roof's edge. The pain caused her to push away while grabbing for a hold, and before she knew it, she was dangling from the edge, facing the building. She didn't have a clue as to what was behind her.

Valerie looked down and saw that she had about 20 feet to drop. She looked left, she looked right. There was no better place to fall that she could see. Her fingers were beginning to slip and they burned with heat and tension. This was not Casey's best idea. She let go with her right hand and tried to swing around a bit to see what was behind her, but the weight was too much for her left arm.

Valerie let go.

She went down.

Straight down.

Bending her knees to lessen the impact, Valerie hit the ground feet-first. She made it. She felt the crunch on the sandy beach shoot up through her body and she made a mental note to reconsider next time someone offered her a vacation.

As she stood up, she still faced the building. She straightened, and it took a few seconds to register that she was looking straight into another small, hollow window...straight into the eyes of the bald native.

Valerie screamed and gasped at the same time and heard the whining native shout something that must have meant "Get her!" because that's exactly what the bald native did. He shoved his arms through the hollow window and firmly grabbed her upper arms. Valerie screamed again in surprise. She hadn't even had a chance to get away.

For what seemed like an eternity, the two just stared at each other. Valerie was still breathing heavily from her rush down the rooftop and the native breathed heavily from anger. "Ooy era oohw!!" the bald native shouted. "Ooy era oohw!!"

The native behind him whined about something else, and suddenly Valerie heard a thump behind her—and then she felt warm breath on the back of her neck. She closed her eyes and gulped. She barely had time to think. Where in the world was—

Casey moved out from behind her and held out one of the vines he had collected earlier. In an instant, he wrapped it around the bald native's left arm, pulling tight. The native grunted and let go of Valerie in protest, trying to get free. Valerie leapt back and gave Casey a quick hug. He had scaled over the building to save her.

Anger spurred Baldy on and he yanked and pulled at his bound wrist, but Casey pulled tighter and tighter. Inside, Whiner ran toward another large door—at the back of the building, near where Casey and Valerie stood. Valerie ran from the building as fast as she could, shouting for Casey to follow her. Instead, he went straight for the door, too, and reached it first. He quickly twisted the other end of the vine around the bottom of one of the logs making up the door. When the whining native reached the door, he pushed hard and Baldy (connected by the vine) was pulled forward, slamming his face into the wall above the small window. Whiner pulled and pushed twice more and Baldy slammed against the wall again and again, shouting with each blow. His eyes filled with anger, as he was most likely thinking about giving his friend something to *really* whine about when he got free.

Frustrated, Whiner ran back toward the front of the building. He was coming over. Valerie ran farther into the boat yard, dodging wooden boats beached in the sand.

"Casey!" she cried. But he wasn't moving. He was just smiling.

Fa-TWANNNNGGG!

Valerie heard the snap before she heard the shout as she watched Whiner vault into the air, caught in one of Casey's tight-vine boar slings. He sailed high into the trees and moments later came back down, pleading for help from god Goofyguy.

"Ha-ha!" Valerie shouted. Casey giggled.

"Let's find that boat," she ordered, excited that their plan was working. The boat yard was in a hidden section of the sandy Jungle Island beach. As Casey said, it was covered with nearly 100 boats, all different shapes and sizes. Several had the evidence of repair work on them, while others were still being built. There were no docks, but the soft tide had created several indentations in the sand which appeared to be used as inlets and launch sites. The other end of the beach was not guarded by a garage station like the side from which they entered. Instead, it simply turned into a swampy jungle route, no doubt too difficult to navigate through. Valerie understood why Casey had brought her the way he did.

Quickly, but carefully, Valerie jogged through the boat yard, ahead of Casey, searching for the two-person boat he had described to her earlier. It was the one boat he had built, and the one boat they knew was seaworthy enough to traverse them the full two miles northeast to Calypso Island.

"Val!" Casey shouted. She whipped her head around toward Casey. The urgency of his voice scared her. There was fright in his eyes. Neither one was feeling as brave as she had hoped. He was pointing behind her. Another native?

When Valerie turned around to look, she wished it *had* been just another native. But it was worse. It was something grayish-green...and it was emerging from the swamp.

"Even if I walk through the valley of the shadow of death, I will fear no evil, for you are with me..." Valerie whispered, remembering the exact words from Psalm 23 that her mother used to quote to her when she was just a little girl. At night, when her mother would draw the sheet separating Valerie's room from the rest of the hut, Valerie would cry and scream, fiercely afraid of the dark. A lot of children have felt afraid of the dark at one time or another in their lives, but with Valerie it seemed to stick a long time. To her, it seemed like more than just a "phase."

To combat the fear, Valerie's mother would sometimes stay in the room with Valerie until she finally fell asleep. As Valerie's eyelids grew heavy, her mother would sing a simple chorus or softly speak a prayer, always based on those verses in Psalm 23:

The Lord is my shepherd. I shall not be in want.

He makes me lie down in green pastures, He leads me beside quiet waters, He restores my soul.

He guides me in the paths of righteousness for his name's sake.

Even though I walk through the valley of the shadow of death,

I will fear no evil, for you are with me.
Your rod and your staff, they comfort me.
You prepare a table before me in the
presence of my enemies.
You anoint my head with oil, my cup overflows.
Surely goodness and love will follow me all
the days of my life.
And I will dwell in the house of the Lord forever.

Over the years, the poetic verses from God's Word became a comfort to Valerie and for the past four years at Superkid Academy, she was able to go to sleep with her room pitch black. What was the difference? Honestly, Valerie had to admit, it was partly because her roommate, Missy, was there with her. Valerie prayed prayers, confessed scripture—she knew God's Word better than any of the other Superkids in her squad. But this giant of fear still loomed before her.

Like a termite, fear kept sneaking out of the cracks, surprising Valerie that it was still in her life. Every time she thought she had terminated it with just the "right" prayer, just the perfect display of boldness, it showed up again—creeping out of the woodwork. It was a giant she threw rocks at, a giant she even managed to knock out at times...but it always got back up off the mat and came for more. And the next time it was stronger. More sinister. More evil.

In a flash, Valerie wondered if she had ever really made the kind of commitment to God she knew was necessary to defeat the fear. Sure, she was a strong Christian. Sure, she was an overcomer. Sure, one day she would be a commander at the Academy. But in order to get rid of the giant—the looming termite of fear—she suddenly realized she would have to let God tear the house down. In order to gain a new life completely free and completely victorious, she would have to let God bring down her old way of living and build her a new one. A firmer foundation. Stronger support beams. And no termites.

The caiman crocodile slithered out of the swamp, covered in moldy-green swamp plants. Its wide eyes blinked once and it snapped viciously. Its crooked teeth glistened in the sunlight, making them look longer and sharper than life. Valerie stared at the crocodile.

"Father God," she whispered, not taking her eyes off the crocodile, "I refuse to just 'try' anymore. I'm making a decision now. I refuse to be afraid. I give You total control of my life. From now on, I'm not going to try and solve everything myself. I'm going to rely upon *You*—*Your* wisdom, *Your* anointing, *Your* power, *Your* will. Fear cannot have hold of me if You're in control. For in 1 John 4:16 it says that You are love. And in 1 John 4:18 it says Your perfect love drives out fear. So, with You in me, fear can't even stay nearby. My life is Yours, Lord. It's really Yours!"

The crocodile snapped again, obviously angry at Valerie's intrusion upon its territory. And Valerie shuddered...but not from a flinch of fear. She shuddered as the revelation of God's love, power and anointing permeated her being. She felt a cool wave of cleansing brushing her body from inside out, from head to foot. Like a current of electricity, fear was forced out of her body as faith filled its place.

But the 10-foot-long crocodile didn't give up. It wasn't aware of her spiritual renewal. All it was aware of was its thin, growling stomach, extremely hungry for something (or someone) to fill it. It drew closer to Valerie, inch by slithering inch. Valerie heard Casey shout from the side that he saw his boat—it was right behind her.

No longer trembling and finally able to think clearly, Valerie surveyed the area. Behind her, on the shoreline, the boat Casey motioned toward rocked in the dark, turquoise ocean water. A quick study of the vessel proved that it had a particularly high rim. If she could make it to it, she could get inside and the crocodile would have a difficult time getting to her. It would be good protection. She was going to go for it.

"P-leeeeeeeeeee-aaaaaahhhhh!" Valerie and the crocodile both turned to the south to look at the Manwan who shouted. It was Whiner, swinging upside down, shouting a distinct call, over and over. Valerie and the crocodile turned their heads to the north as they heard a series of sudden splashes in the water. Valerie wasn't sure what it was, but she didn't want to stick around and

find out. For all she knew, it was Al E. Gator's family wanting to join in the fun.

Seeing the crocodile still distracted with curiosity, Valerie swung around and broke into a 100-foot sprint to Casey's boat. The sand shoved in its face angered the reptile and it took off after her at full speed. Valerie's disadvantage was her footing on the sand. Three-fourths of the way there, the crocodile nipped her heels. A swift foot-slam in the sand blew another gritty mouthful of beach pebbles into her adversary's face. It recoiled temporarily—long enough for Valerie to take a flying leap to the rocking vessel.

She landed on top and pulled her feet inside, quickly avoiding losing her toes to the meat eater. *BAM! CRACK!* The crocodile's nose slammed against the underside of the boat as it unsuccessfully attempted to stop in its tracks. Its tail whipped around in anger and it let out a low, deep, hissing sound.

The boat rocked in the water and Valerie attempted to steady it. She didn't want it to flip over, trapping her underneath with an angry crocodile for company. The boat slid backward into the ocean water, rocking even more. As it rocked to the right, something slid out from underneath the board-bench Valerie was perched on. She reached down to grab it, but then froze. It moved. No, it slithered.

Tss-ss-ss-ss-ss-ss-ss...

She wanted to jump out to avoid a bite from the familiar-looking tropical rattlesnake, but realized that would mean a tangle with the crocodile, which was even less promising. Coming straight toward her, shouting, Casey was hopping from boat to boat, avoiding the sandy territory of the crocodile.

The boat Valerie occupied was drifting backward, rolling farther away from the island. The snake was coiling beneath her. The crocodile was splashing and lurking near. Casey was only one boat away.

With a push that made his calf muscles bulge, Casey launched off the last boat and flew to Valerie.

"Watch out for the snake!" Valerie screamed. But the snake was the least of Casey's troubles. He curled his legs up to his body as he soared through the air. The crocodile snapped up, trying to get a snack, but Casey was clear. He landed right in the boat, directly behind Valerie, almost causing the vessel to capsize. Valerie worked to steady it, never taking her eyes off the snake.

Casey leaned forward when he heard the snake hiss.

"Hallo, snake!" he greeted the reptile, reaching for it.

"Casey, no!!!"

The young boy grabbed the olive snake at its neck, lifted it up and threw it at the crocodile. The tropical rattlesnake hissed, bounced off the thick bridge between the crocodile's eyes and slithered away at record speed. The startled caiman crocodile went berserk, unsure of what hit him. It instantly vacated the premises as well, retreating into the swamp.

Valerie's brown eyes were wide, taking it all in. Casey was cooling down, working to catch his breath. Valerie wasn't sure what to say.

"Casey...you could have...the snake...poisonous... why...thank you."

"No problem. Cayseilauphlan taught how to catch snakes. Cayseilauphlan make you one sometime."

"Make me one? You mean to *eat?!*"

Casey affirmed her suspicion with a nod of his head.

"No, *thanks.* I've had my fill of snakes for a lifetime."

Their boat slowly drifted out into the ocean and each adventurer picked up an oar from inside the boat. They began to paddle their way northward. As they moved in silence, tired from their trials, Valerie began to realize it was over.

They had escaped merciless natives, a hissing rattle-snake, a hungry crocodile—and that was all within less than an hour. This had been some vacation. Valerie couldn't wait to get back to Superkid Academy where she could have a decent rest—and a shower. She still felt disgusting.

Casey looked back over his shoulder at her and smiled. Valerie giggled. Casey chuckled. Then together they began to laugh. They had done it. They had escaped Jungle Island. What else could *possibly* go wrong?

Bloop.

Bloop-bloop.

Bloop-bloop-bloop.

Valerie stopped laughing long enough to take note of the sudden gurgling sound she heard. What now— sharks? Stingrays? A school of piranhas?

Bloop-bloop-bloop-bloop-bloop-bloop-bloop-bloop-bloop-bloop...

The boat's captain was pointing to the floor. Valerie followed the trail of Casey's finger and couldn't believe her eyes. They were 50 feet from shore and a little spring of water was popping up through a crack in the bottom of the boat. A present from Al the crocodile. At the current flooding rate, they'd probably make it halfway to Calypso. That, of course, wouldn't do them much good.

"We have to go back." Valerie couldn't believe what she was saying. They had to head back to the angry natives, the tropical rattlesnake and the hungry crocodile. They didn't have a choice.

"Look!" Casey shouted, pointing at the ocean water ahead of them. Tiny sticks of bamboo were sticking straight out.

"Paddle backward!" Valerie cried. "We don't want to hit them! We don't need anything hitting us now!"

They both reversed the direction of their paddling. Splashing water filled the air around them. The sound reminded Valerie of the noise she had heard when she'd first faced the crocodile. Some kind of splashing sound...what *was* that, anyway?

They quickly retreated.

"No wait! Stop again! More bamboo!" Behind them were more menacing sticks of bamboo poking up from the water. Funny, Valerie didn't remember them being there earlier...

They paddled on one side of the canoe, spinning it around to fire off in another direction. But when they were finally turned and ready to go, there were more bamboo sticks in front of them.

"Wait!" Valerie shouted, used to taking control from her hours co-piloting SuperCopters. "Something's wrong here."

The two young adventurers looked around them and discovered that they were completely surrounded by the little bamboo sticks. There was nowhere they could go. And their feet were slowly being slapped with water trickling in from the tiny crack in the bottom of the boat.

They waited for a moment, trying to come up with a plan. Trying to find a way of escape. They waited. And they thought.

Spa-LOOSH! Up from the ocean water, 30 men rose in unison, each one holding a dripping spear in his hand and a hollow, bamboo stick in his mouth. Their sudden appearance shocked Valerie and Casey and they both jumped in surprise. Each of their captors was covered in the familiar, white, Manwan markings.

"Evom t'nod!" one yelled. Valerie looked at Casey. He didn't move a muscle. Baldy's call into the jungle and the splashing she'd heard made sense now. They had been secretly moving in all this time— underwater—to capture her and Casey. Even if there hadn't been a crocodile, a rattlesnake or crack in their boat, they wouldn't have gotten far. Suddenly Valerie realized whether they liked it or not, they were about to go back to good, old Jungle Island.

The Manwan camp was deeply hidden inside Jungle Island's natural growth. In fact, unless someone was distinctly looking for it, it would be easy to miss entirely. But once inside, an adventurer would discover a whole village filled with several hundred families—men, women, children, teenagers, and even a few pet monkeys.

The tiny village was desperately primitive and magnificently advanced at the same time. The men and boys were dressed as Casey was, with gray cloths around their waists and white markings on their faces and chests. The women and girls wore simple gray cloths stretching from their chests down to their knees. They were barefoot like the males, but didn't wear the distinct Manwan markings.

The citizens lived in camouflaged, grass-and-mud huts that seemed to disappear into the jungle when you weren't looking for them. Valerie noted that they didn't seem as solid as the boat yard building had been, but the units were close together, providing a degree of protection. The only mode of ground transportation was by foot. Meanwhile, above the village and throughout the trees, a system of ropes and pulleys held wooden boxcars that slid from one side of the village to another in a quarter of the time it would take to walk.

When they entered under the guard of the 30 proud natives, the first thing Valerie noticed was that she wasn't afraid anymore. As she placed her hope and trust in the Lord, faith replaced the fear that she would have experienced only hours earlier...before she put her complete trust in her Savior.

Through eyes devoid of fear, the Manwans didn't seem merciless and uncivil at all. There were families eating together, citizens bartering for one another's goods, and children running and playing beneath the tall jungle trees. The Manwans didn't appear to be a bad people or even a mean people. They were only a deceived people, serving a god that didn't exist, hoping to one day find true fulfillment in life...to find true meaning. Valerie knew the Manwans would only find those things in Jesus. And right now, she was possibly closer than any other man or woman had ever been to the Manwans...alive, anyway.

She knew she'd have to be cautious. She realized her life depended on it. She understood that they may not want to listen. But as she strolled through the village at spearpoint, a deep, searing compassion burned in her heart. She thought of the words she had read before in Matthew 9:36, about how when Jesus saw the crowds, He was moved with compassion "because they were hurting and helpless, like sheep without a shepherd." Valerie understood now how Jesus must have felt. He boldly walked into strange lands. Many times, people didn't want Him or the miracle of life He freely offered. But He never gave up. And Valerie decided to follow His example.

"Val, no fear." Casey was beside Valerie as they marched in. He lifted up a comforting hand and wiped a runaway tear from Valerie's cheek. On reflex, Valerie wiped beneath both of her eyes and brushed the tears away. But she knew that with the dust on her face from their adventure, the small tear trails wouldn't disappear.

"I'm not fearful," Valerie softly assured her friend. "I just can't help it. I finally realized why Satan has tried to keep me afraid of the dark all these years. He's wanted to make sure I'm too scared to go into the jungle—too scared to enter the places that make me uneasy. Places like this are all over the world. And he knows that inside them there are hundreds of people— good people—deceived and living without ever knowing Jesus. He's kept me so scared that I never would have gone to them...and I never would have truly followed the dream God put in my heart..."

"What Val dream?" Casey's question stirred Valerie's heart as they walked.

"When I was little, I wanted to be a missionary. But as I've grown older, God has shown me that one day I'll be a commander at Superkid Academy. But I realize something else now, too. I realize that God has *also* put a desire within me to reach people like this...God wants *everyone* to reach people like this...no matter what their life's dream is. This is part of it."

Casey didn't respond, but kept marching. Valerie wasn't sure he completely understood what she was saying or feeling. She withdrew her emotions, realizing it wasn't the time to let tears fall. But still the compassion penetrated her entire being so that it was almost more than she could bear. Casey must have noticed her struggle because he began to give her a brief tour as they walked, attempting to help her get her mind off the situation.

"Those 'reylf's,'" Casey was pointing to the boxcars in the trees.

"They're fast," Valerie noted. Casey nodded. Then he pointed to a group of young men and women playing some kind of game with gigantic leaves and a large, round nut. They were blowing the nut around with gusts of air created by waving the leaves. Most were giggling and carrying on. A few watched Valerie and Casey, looking as if they were sad to see them arrive.

"Those Cayseilauphlan friends. We learn English from Manwan leader together."

"Does everyone in the village know English?" Valerie wondered.

"No, only Manwan leader and leader's students."

"Hmm."

As they continued through the busy village, Casey pointed out more friends, unusual structures and the significance of several buildings. Up ahead, set apart from the rest of the Manwan tribal structures, three large buildings stood, finer and more detailed than all the rest. They were all created with long tree trunks, like the boat yard building, and they all had the same sharply angled roofs. Each of these buildings, however, had open entrances and several hollow, front windows. All were a single story and easily several hundred square feet in size.

To Valerie's left, a thin podium carved with intertwined fish and serpents stood outside the first building. An open pit lay far in front of it, with black sear marks spread over the ground.

The building on the right side had distinct wood carvings in the specially designed, arched doorway. On the bottom of the right side, a figure was carved. Above the figure, an arrow pointing up led to a starburst at the top. Standing directly in front of this building was a large, wooden statue of a man-like bird. His feet had talons, his arms and back were covered with feathers and his face was like a hawk. Glaring. Piercing. Determined. But the expression was more than that. It was also merciless.

Beneath the statue lay fresh food, gift baskets and homemade items. Valerie noticed that all the footprints leading up to the statue were facing forward...as though those who brought the gifts walked up, placed them down and then retreated, never turning around or taking their eyes off the statue until they were a safe distance away.

The center building was wider than the other two, and quite majestic in appearance. A stone walkway led to the square doorway. In each stone was carved a feather and each feather was dyed a different color. In a village filled with browns and greens, the stones stood out brilliantly. It was directly in front of this building that Valerie and Casey's escort stopped. To their left was the pulpit and the pit and to their right was the statue.

Valerie felt an eeriness fill the air as the soldiers surrounding them stepped back and bowed their heads in unison. The native soldier in the front of the group shouted a few words Valerie didn't understand and then moved aside and bowed his head also. Valerie looked to Casey for an explanation, but he wasn't looking at her. He was staring straight ahead at the center building.

Out from the doorway an older, muscular, dark man emerged. He was wearing a cloth like the other tribe members, but also had the luxury of a short vest made of multicolored feathers. Deep reds, purples, blues, greens and yellows brought a stark contrast to the rest of the plain-looking Manwan tribe members. His expression was nonchalant, yet his presence demanded respect and authority. He traversed the walkway of stones, to the entourage surrounding Valerie and Casey. A pathway opened in the group, allowing the leader closer to the captives.

He looked at Valerie and Casey closely and then lifted up his arms. The soldiers' heads stayed bowed.

From the right and left buildings, two more commanding natives emerged, though each was dressed in different attire. Each was aged, but not as much as the first man who emerged. The man from the left-hand building was weightier and wore a simple cloth like the other Manwans. Nothing special. The man from the right-hand building, on the other hand, was very thin and wore a robe instead, vanilla in color, draped down to his toes. The two men each took their places behind the first man and awaited further instruction.

The head man was silent for a moment as he looked Valerie over. Then he turned to Casey and looked disappointed.

"Ereh gniod ooy era tahw?!" the man demanded of Casey. Casey softly spoke some Manwan words back. The man huffed.

"So you speak English?"

Valerie was shocked to hear the familiar words come from the Manwan man. "Wha—you—what?"

"You speak English?" he repeated, glaring at Valerie. She tried hard to move as little as possible. She didn't want to risk being disrespectful.

"Yes, sir. I do," she replied. "My name is Valerie Rivera. I come from Calypso Island."

The man's features softened. "I am Honcho, the Manwan leader. You're a long way from home, Valerie Rivera. Why have you invaded our homeland?"

Valerie looked at Casey and swallowed hard. He didn't return her look.

"With all respect, sir, I didn't mean to invade. I'm lost. But now I see that it may be the Lord's plan for me to be here. I have a message for you."

Casey suddenly looked up at Valerie. He was obviously shocked at her boldness, almost as much as Valerie was herself.

The man on the left side of the leader leaned in and whispered something unintelligible in his ear. The leader's eyes narrowed. He looked at Casey's handband with the picture of the skull. Then his eyes met Casey's.

"You have been banned from this tribe, Cayseilauphlan. Why have you dared to risk infecting us with your disease?"

Valerie wasn't sure why he was speaking to Casey in English, but she imagined it was to humiliate him in front of her.

"C-Cayseilauphlan sorry," Casey muttered. "I help Val. That all."

The leader turned back to Valerie. He reached a hand forward and brushed a thin layer of dust off her shoulder.

"You are a pretty girl," he said. "Only because you are young and Cayseilauphlan risked his life as well as yours, I will listen to your message." The thin man in the robe scowled and tightened his lips.

"Here is the message I bring," Valerie began. "I serve the God above all gods, the Lord Jesus Christ—

and He wants to be Your Lord today. He loves you and He wants to bring you victory."

The robed man tapped the Manwan leader on the shoulder. He whispered something harshly and the leader spoke back. The man spoke again and Honcho turned back to Valerie.

"This is our spiritual chief. He says any words a stranger brings are lies...because strangers want to steal away our power—the power we receive from worshiping our god, Guphigai." Honcho pointed toward the wooden man/hawk statue.

So that's Goofyguy, Valerie thought. *He does look goofy...*

"You worship that statue?" Valerie wondered aloud. The leader nodded.

"Guphigai protects us," Honcho explained. "He helps or punishes us as he sees fit. Do you dare to challenge Guphigai's power?"

A flash went through Valerie's mind. She remembered the Old Testament story of Elijah, who proved God's power by challenging the false gods. Of course, God showed His might and made believers of the doubting. She remembered the story of Moses, who challenged Pharaoh to free God's people. When Pharaoh wouldn't, Moses showed God's mighty power time and again as proof. Now Valerie felt like she was in the same situation.

"No, I won't challenge Goofyguy," Valerie said, letting her new name for the god slip on purpose. "I won't challenge him because it wouldn't be fair. He has no power. Not real power. But I serve a God Who is *all-powerful*." Valerie remembered what Casey had said about the Manwans. "He can free you from your fears. He can protect you and He will bless you. Jesus said He is the only way, truth and life. To get to the Father—the God above all gods—you must go through Him. *He* is the true God. And *He* is the One Whom I serve."

The leader frowned and scoffed. "You act like the One. You stand so bold and sure," he spat. "But a young girl? Threatening our god? Threatening the Manwans? You bring Guphigai's judgment upon yourself."

"What do you mean, I 'act like the One'?" Valerie asked, unafraid.

The leader pointed to the archway of the building housing the "spiritual chief," the witch doctor. Valerie looked at the carving of the man who turned into a star-burst. The leader explained.

"Long ago, a prophet came to the Manwan land and told us that One would come who would introduce us to true power and true wisdom. It is for the hope of meeting that One that I have learned many languages and taught them to some of my students. We have prepared ourselves for any visitor."

Valerie shook her head. She was astonished at the boldness rising up within her, but she also knew this may be her only chance to reason with the merciless Manwans. "Honcho, I *serve* the God with true power and true wisdom. I may not be the One you expect, but let me speak to your people. Let me—"

The robed man, the witch doctor, shouted something to the leader in Manwan and the man on Honcho's other side shouted something back. Honcho silenced them both by raising his hands.

"Valerie Rivera. You have trespassed on Manwan territory. You have dared to threaten our god. You will stand trial before Guphigai."

"Trial?" Valerie couldn't believe her ears. This was like something out of a science-fiction movie.

"This evening, as the light of the sun descends, you will be put on trial for trespassing and deceit. We will offer you two identical bags. By the choice you make between the two bags, Guphigai will determine your destiny. If you choose the bag filled with feathers, you will go free. If you choose the one containing snake rattles, you will become an instant sacrifice to Guphigai. May your 'God' give you wisdom."

Valerie was speechless. This sounded ridiculous. Absurd. Primitive. And yet her life was on the line. The leader and his two companions ended the conversation abruptly by turning around in unison and heading for their respective buildings.

"Val, *now* good time to fear," Casey whispered. "Very bad. Cayseilauphlan sorry."

"Oh, no, it's not your fault, Casey," Valerie touched his arm softly, not taking her eyes off the retreating leader. "God's will is going to be done. According to Deuteronomy 30:19, I know God wants me to choose life. I believe He'll help me make that choice. I've put my life in His hands...not the Manwan's."

"Val no fear?" Casey's forehead wrinkled and his eyes searched for the truth.

"Val no fear," Valerie responded confidently, repeating his words. "I am God's child. He is going to take care of me."

"Then Cayseilauphlan serve Val God. He make Cayseilauphlan strong, too."

Hope leaped up inside Valerie. Casey was seeing the light. "I know He will," she promised, squeezing his arm.

The leader suddenly stopped and turned around before entering his palace. He barked an order to a couple warriors. They lifted their heads and harshly grabbed Casey, escorting him away. Valerie shot a concerned glance at the leader and caught a sorrowful glance of his own. Then he hardened.

"Where are they taking him?" Valerie demanded, sticking up for her friend.

"Back to the jungle," the leader responded with force. "Manwan will not kill Manwan. We will let him go, to live the best life he can on his own. But we cannot allow him to stay with us. He will infect the others. We used to be thousands. Now we are only hundreds because of disease like his. We must not risk losing more."

Valerie understood. It was the only thing they knew to do. They were afraid. And now it was time for her to do the only thing she knew to do. She had to pray.

Valerie wasn't surprised that they had kept her away from the leader's building and the Manwan temple. But she was surprised when they escorted her into the first building. Apparently, Valerie reasoned, she had been led into the justice building of the Manwan tribe. She was only escorted into the front entrance, though, where she saw various signs she figured to be laws and rulings. She even thought she saw a corner filled with bones of trespassers, but then she imagined her mind was just playing tricks on her.

The three warriors shoved her into a large, nearly empty room at the front of the structure. It was the holding area. The jail. The room was lit by a small system of perfectly angled, square holes in the top of the ceiling. Sunlight shot small, crude beams onto the dusty floor. There was a wooden cot on the far side and a small washbasin standing next to it. Underneath the basin, two colorful jugs and a small basket filled with knickknacks looked out of place. The guards shut a heavy, log door behind her and barred it—but not before handing her a thickly folded cloth.

Valerie suddenly felt very alone again. She unfolded the cloth the guards had given her. Keeping busy helped her forget about everything for a moment. She softly prayed in the spirit.

The cloth unfolded into the shape of a large blanket. Apparently they wanted her to be nice and rested for her execution. She walked over to the bed, dropped the blanket on top and moved to the basin. It was clean and smooth and made from thick, polished wood. At its foot stood two large jugs; one was empty and the other was filled to the rim with water. Valerie carefully lifted the weighty water jug and poured some of the clear liquid into the basin. It filled up completely before she'd even poured half the water out. The water was chilly.

Valerie fumbled through the basket and found a jar of crushed leaves that smelled like soapy grass. She poured some into the basin and mixed them with the water. The result was a cold basin of soap suds. She parted the suds once as she mixed and saw her reflection in the cool water. She couldn't believe how filthy she looked. Mud-caked, dirt-ridden, dust-covered, sand-blown. But, then again, that's how she felt. Even her hair was coarse. Valerie grabbed the bed blanket and decided it would serve much better as a washcloth and towel.

Without the slightest hesitation, Valerie dunked her whole head into the basin. Her hair immediately loosened and dirt swam out. Valerie raised up and scrubbed the soapy water into her hair. Before rinsing, she scooped out most of the dirty water with the empty jug, then refilled the basin with more clean water. Then she closed her eyes and dunked again to rinse the soap out of her hair. Valerie squeezed the long strands into little clumps to get all the water out. The basin was filthy again, so she scooped the water out once more and started over.

The cool water on her skin felt like a summer breeze after the rain. Her stomach muscles retracted when she touched her burn with the wet blanket, but the stinging seemed to soothe. Moments later, she had completed washing her arms and face. Nearly all the water evaporated before she even had a chance to dry herself with the other end of the sheet.

Her tank top appeared clean enough after a bit of scrubbing with the soapy water. Valerie twisted the edge of her shirt over the basin, wringing out the excess water. The remaining coolness in the cloth felt great against her adventure-torn skin. With her hair slowly curling after its washing, Valerie thumped down on the cot.

What a day.

What a vacation.

"Even if I walk through the valley of the shadow of death, I will fear no evil, for you are with me." Valerie said it aloud. The words echoed in the large chamber. Those words meant something now. It wasn't just Valerie against the world any more. Now she had God Almighty on her side. Sure, she always knew that, but now she truly realized her life was not her own—it was His. She thought about this over and over. She didn't quite understand how she could be so relaxed before such a trying time.

That's the peace that passes understanding, the Holy Spirit reminded her of Philippians 4:7. Valerie smiled.

"Lord, I lift Casey up to You," she prayed, thinking of her friend before herself. "I pray according to John 10:10 that he'd walk in the abundant life he desires. He doesn't have a church or even any friends who can help him. I pray that You would teach him. Bring someone across his path who can minister life to him. Show him he's not alone. Show him he's not a lost cause. And I continue to thank You for the healing we've prayed for him to receive." Valerie slipped off the bed and knelt on the ground. This was her favorite way to pray at home— leaning on her bed, with her hands folded. For now, the bare, wooden cot would have to do.

"I also pray for my mom, my dad, Rapper, Commander Kellie and the other Superkids. I join my faith with theirs. I'm sure they're praying for me right now. And You said in Matthew 18:19-20 that when we agree together, what we ask will be done, for You are with us. I stand on that today.

"And, Father God, in Jesus' Name, I pray for the wisdom Your Word says we can ask for in James 1:5. I thank You for giving it to me. Show me what to do when I'm faced with my decision. Show me which bag to pick. God, my life is Yours. I believe as Psalm 118:17

says, I will not die but live, and will proclaim what the Lord has done.

"Finally, I pray for the Manwans. Lord, they're deceived by Satan. Therefore, according to Matthew 16:19, I bind Satan from interfering. I come against the powers that are over this tribe and I cast them down, in Jesus' Name."

Valerie continued to pray in the spirit, bringing her prayers to God by letting the Holy Spirit pray through her in the special language God had given her. When she opened her eyes, peace persisted and she noticed the room wasn't as bright. The sun would be going down soon, and at that time, she would have to stand before the Manwans and boldly show them which one she had chosen: life or death.

A single sunbeam shone on Valerie's folded hands. At first, Valerie thought it was from the ceiling, but then she realized it was actually coming from the front wall. She leaned forward and peered into it. It was a small hole, bored in the wooden wall, no doubt by an earlier captive who may have had the same choice...a captive who probably never returned.

Valerie looked out and could see many Manwan natives setting out logs for a fire, painting their bodies and setting up the site of the judgment. Valerie watched as the heavy Manwan judge, who had stood at the leader's left side, arrived with two identical snakeskin bags. He set them on the wooden podium carved with intertwined fish and serpents.

They were the bags filled with feathers and rattles.

They were the bags that would determine her future.

Valerie sat back, but felt a sudden urgency to keep watch. At first, she almost mistook it for hunger, but she had had the feeling before. It was the Holy Spirit prompting her about something. She willingly obeyed and leaned up to the hole again. When she did, she saw the judge was gone. Now the witch doctor was walking—no, sneaking—up to the podium. Carefully scanning the area around him, he opened both bags. Quickly, he picked one of the bags up and switched it with an identical-looking snakeskin bag at his side. Valerie noticed a small, white feather whisk out of the bag he removed.

What is he doing?

The lanky man grabbed the feather that dropped and stuffed it back in the bag. Then, still carefully looking around him, he adjusted the bags on the podium, pulling a handful of the contents out of each to double-check his work. Both handfuls were filled with snake rattles. Valerie gasped and sat back against the bed.

No wonder no one had ever escaped from Jungle Island. The witch doctor was fixing it so that the Manwans would never hear about the gospel. He was fixing it so Guphigai would always be their god. He was fixing it so no matter which bag Valerie picked, she would come up with snake rattles...and become Guphigai's immediate sacrifice.

▲   ▲   ▲

The sun was lowering and the air was crisp. Native guards had come to retrieve Valerie and bring her to her trial. When they marched her outside, she was amazed at the extensive preparations the tribe had gone through to witness the event. Instead of the standard white Manwan markings, men and women alike were marked with brilliant reds, greens, blues and yellows. Many were dancing and chanting, looking remarkably like a scene in a cliché-ish Hollywood movie. In front of her stood the wooden podium of judgment displaying the two identical, olive snakeskin bags. Beyond it was where most of the celebrating was taking place around a mammoth bonfire, dispersing an astounding amount of heat. Valerie felt it warm her up instantly.

She peered into the fire and noticed a stone pillar shooting up from the middle. No doubt, the sacrificial stake Valerie would be forced to take if she chose the wrong bag...or *any* bag, in her case.

Resonating drum beats were drowned out only by chanting and an occasional war whoop. Valerie was escorted directly in front of the podium and held at spearpoint. She stood, awaiting her judgment.

She could feel fear working at her, trying to sink its claws into her.

God's not going to save you. You're going to become a sacrifice just like anyone else who has ever entered Manwan territory. Who do you think you are, saying what you did to the leader?

Valerie looked around her. At first, she thought someone had spoken to her...but then she realized the voice had been silent. Fear was working double time to gain a hold.

"The Lord is on my side; I will not fear," Valerie whispered, quoting Psalm 118:6.

She looked at the bright orange fire. The heat caused her to begin perspiring.

There is no hope for you, Valerie.

"My trust and hope are in the Lord," she responded with Jeremiah 17:7. She could hear the crackling wood. The thick, rank smell of smoke filled her nostrils. She turned her head away quickly, forcing herself not to think about anything contrary to the promises of God.

"I cast down every power of darkness and every thought that would try to make me stumble. I will see the salvation of the Lord today!"

Valerie looked above her, into the trees. She couldn't see the sky, but somehow just the act of looking up brought comfort. Soft beams of fading light still filtered through the leaves.

She continued speaking scriptures she had memorized, stirring up her faith, as she watched a wooden boxcar quickly scoot overhead. She wished for a moment that she had wings so she could fly up to it and be whisked away to safety. But the reylf, as Casey had called it, scooted on and she stayed put. No wings today.

The drum beating, dancing, chanting and whooping suddenly stopped when Honcho, the Manwan leader, emerged from his quarters. He held both his hands up and the judge and witch doctor stood at his sides. Together they marched forward and took their places on the opposite sides of the podium. Valerie was directly across from them.

The leader shouted something and the Manwan crowd responded in unison. Valerie had no idea what they were saying. The ritual repeated several times until finally the leader looked Valerie straight in the eyes and began speaking English.

"This is your trial, Valerie Rivera. May Guphigai determine your fate. Should you choose the bag containing feathers, you shall go free. Should you choose the bag with the rattles, you shall become a sacrifice to our great god."

The Manwan leader didn't waste any more time or words. He simply nodded at the two bags before Valerie and held out his hands, indicating for her to make a choice. Confidently, Valerie reached out for a bag, grabbed it and held it above her head. She heard it rattle as it swooped by her ear. With all the boldness she could muster, she proclaimed, "My faith is in the Lord God

Almighty, Creator of the universe! Today you will see the salvation of the Lord!"

Her words echoed in the forest camp and it became so silent, Valerie felt like she could have heard a pin drop. The eyes of the witch doctor narrowed as he sneered. The judge frowned. Honcho's lips tightened. The Manwans stared at her blankly. The fire crackled hot on her back. And the statue of Guphigai glistened in the firelight.

The leader barely moved his lips as he asked, "Is that your choice?"

The surge of boldness and strength Valerie felt began to rest. She glanced at the bag she held in her hand and then began to lower it.

Valerie nodded.

The witch doctor grinned menacingly. He knew he had won. No matter which bag Valerie picked, she was destined to become another meaningless sacrifice to Guphigai.

But Valerie was operating in faith—not fear. She knew her God—the King of the universe, the Creator of all, the God above all gods—would not let her down. If He could create a man out of the dust of the earth like the Bible said, He could most certainly perform a miracle. He could turn those rattles into feathers. He was the *true* God.

Honcho motioned the witch doctor forward. With another sneer and an evil smile, he reached out to take the bag from Valerie. She almost let go when an alarm went off in her spirit, like a flashing sign in the darkest of night. She saw the look in his eyes. He was going to double-cross her. Even if God changed the rattles to feathers, he wasn't going to tell the leader the truth. Because if she were allowed to live, Guphigai would be challenged...and the witch doctor would lose his respect. He would lose his job. He wouldn't allow that to happen. Valerie silently asked and thanked the Lord for wisdom again.

That's when the idea hit her.

Valerie tightened her grip on the bag and shouted, "I choose this one!" and then pitched it into the center of the fire. Instantly, the bag disappeared, disintegrating in a blaze of fire and heat. The witch doctor leapt backward, shocked at her behavior. Honcho, the Manwan leader, looked at her, puzzled.

What *was* she doing?

Valerie pointed to the bag still remaining on the podium. "Open it up," she prompted. "Go ahead. If you see snake rattles inside, you'll know I must have picked the one with the feathers...and I must be set *free* according to your laws."

The leader nodded, certainly not fully understanding what was happening. He motioned for the witch doctor to check the bag. The witch doctor looked unsure, not wanting to open it. Honcho said something to him in Manwan and he picked up the bag.

Now the moment of truth!

The witch doctor fumbled with the bag and was so nervous he dropped it. It hit the ground with a soft thump and a rattle. After he picked it back up, he opened the bag, looked inside and re-closed it. He whispered to Honcho. The leader nodded. Valerie could feel her heart beating 100 miles an hour. The witch doctor passed the bag to him and the leader poured its contents onto the judgment podium.

At once, dozens of white feathers drifted onto the wooden surface.

"This bag contains feathers," Honcho announced to Valerie, as the white feathers slowly rested. "You must have picked the bag with rattles. I'm afraid your God hasn't come through. Guphigai has determined your fate."

"*What?!?!*" Valerie panicked. *How could that be?* She *knew* she saw him sabotage the trial. She *knew* she saw him switch the bag of white feathers with the rattles he had carried on his—

His belt. Valerie looked down to see the witch doctor tightening his belt...with an olive snakeskin bag still attached to it. When he dropped the bag seconds ago, he had done it on purpose. He had switched the bag *back.* He'd fooled everyone.

Valerie pointed at him. "He—"

Suddenly the blunt end of a spear knocked her on the back of her shoulders.

"*Ummph!*"

Valerie hit the ground with her knees. The crowd cheered and the Manwan leader announced something in his own language. It must have been her death sentence, for the mass of Manwans began chanting again, this time in unison, as some threw more logs on the fire. Valerie could feel the intensity of the heat increase. She felt defeated.

Where's the salvation of the Lord, Valerie? Where's His rescuing power?

She glanced back at the fire as the guards bound her wrists with rope. She looked at the stone pillar looming in the center. Soon she would be there. Valerie could barely breathe.

Still on her knees, she looked forward and saw the statue of the wooden god, Guphigai, standing there, stiff as a rock. She refused to bow to it. With the last of the strength she could muster, Valerie pushed up off her knees.

A holy anger filled her being as she peered at the witch doctor and proclaimed again, "Even this day you will see the power of the God above all gods to save my life." The witch doctor wouldn't look her in the eye.

Valerie turned around and faced the fire. It was burning hot and threatening. At once, she felt 12 arrowheads on her back. She had no choice—she was being pushed forward. Into the heat. Into the orange flames. Into the fire.

"God is my refuge and my strength. He is an ever-present help in times of trouble. So I will not fear even if the earth gives way and the mountains fall into the heart of the sea, even if its waters roar and foam and the mountains quake—or even if the fire burns," she said aloud, standing on Psalm 46 and marching forward, entering the fire. Valerie was determined to stand on the Word...even to the end. She closed her eyes.

CRACK! SMACK! FLICK! Flames leapt up at her side. The warriors drew back, but Valerie kept walking.

Their spears could no longer reach her. She was in the middle of the fire.

She was in the middle of the fire!

Valerie stopped when she felt the stone pillar in front of her. She opened her eyes. Flames surrounded her. Black smoke flew up in front of her eyes. Hot coals burned at her feet. But she felt nothing. No burning, no pain...only a coolness that covered her from head to toe. She looked down at her clothes and saw how bright they glowed, reflecting the fire around her...yet they weren't burning. Even the leaf-shoe Casey had made her felt cool like metal against the arch of her foot.

The fire was too high to see out, but she could hear the chants of the Manwan tribe slowly drift away as they realized she wasn't burning. She wasn't becoming their sacrifice. She didn't belong to Guphigai. She belonged to God.

Valerie felt warm for the first time when a glowing figure appeared in front of her, brighter than the fire. He was wearing a robe of light that blew slowly, unaffected by the fact that there was no breeze. She couldn't make out his shining face, but she could hear his rumbling voice. It was saying, "You have been faithful; the Lord is pleased."

The Superkid was speechless...and yet entirely peaceful...even in the midst of the fire. Like the Bible story of Shadrach, Meshach and Abednego, she could not be burned! A splash of water hit her arm and she turned to see some Manwans throwing water on the fire.

The logs hissed and smoked as the water snuffed out paths up to where she stood. The figure faded away as quickly as he had appeared, but before he did she heard him give her one last instruction.

"Their hearts are yet hard," he stated. "Now you must run. For the prophecy must be fulfilled."

"Wha—but—but—" The figure shot straight up into the air, bringing a trail of fire with him. The fire trail smacked straight into an empty boxcar flying overhead and lit it up in an instant. The boxcar slid down its path and rolled about 40 yards when, completely a ball of flames, it dropped straight down and smashed on top of the statue of Guphigai. The wooden figure burst into a miniature inferno. Valerie saw the witch doctor's eyes grow wide in shock as he ran to the statue. He was blowing on it, trying to put out the fire. But Goofyguy was toast.

Valerie looked around her. The bonfire was lessening as the buckets of water hit the coals and the logs. Warriors equipped with spears were venturing closer. Apparently they hadn't seen the angelic messenger. They only saw the fact that Valerie wasn't burning. She was beginning to feel the heat of the fire now. It was time to do what the angelic figure told her to do. It was time to run.

▲　▲　▲

Another splash of water formed a perfect path for Valerie to follow out of the fire. Her feet crunched the hissing logs and coals, making her getaway louder than she had hoped. She heard Honcho, the Manwan leader, bark some orders that summoned a small army of Manwan warriors to head in Valerie's direction. As she ran, she looked over her shoulder to see 50 angry Manwans with 50 sharpened spears hot on her trail. Heading the group were Baldy and Whiner...but Valerie wasn't interested in a reunion.

The jungle forest was getting darker now. The light of dusk only allowed her to see about 20 feet ahead. She had no idea where she was heading. She realized as she ran that the Manwans had the greater advantage. They were familiar with the forest. They were familiar with hunting at night. They were greater in number.

Valerie prayed between quick breaths that she wouldn't come upon some hideous form of wildlife that was looking for an early evening snack. She could hear monkeys scream and animals run as their comforts were interrupted by the band of sprinting, shouting warriors.

Valerie looked back over her shoulder again and couldn't see any natives, but she could hear every one of them. They were close. She hoped they couldn't see her either. Quickly she turned back around and—

THUNK!

—she ran right into a tree.

Valerie screamed and huffed, feeling the pain surge through her like an electrical shock. She jumped back up and took off running. Her life depended on it. She felt dizzy. She lost her bearings.

A sudden spear whizzed by her ear and made her sharp again. *Oh, yeah, natives.* The next spear landed between her feet, forcing her to jump when it hit. She heard the spears thunking against tree trunks and swishing through the leaves. Yet not one hit her. She realized the Lord was protecting her; the natives were better shots than that. *The Lord would not bring me this far to forget me,* she thought as the truth of God's faithfulness rose up in her spirit.

But her mental victory seemed short-lived. For she heard something up ahead. Grunting. Snorting. Snarling. And then she saw a flash of grayish-brown in the tall grass. A pack of wild boars. They were coming straight for her. Valerie slammed to a stop and grabbed onto the nearest tree. She looked up. It was too tall to climb quickly. There wasn't enough time to do anything. In a split second the natives would be upon her. In a split second after that, the boars would be charging her. There was nowhere to go. She looked down. Maybe she'd suddenly find a boar trap she could drop into. Maybe she'd find...

What was that?

Twenty feet to her left.

Lying on the ground.

Meticulously wrapped in a circle.

Dangling from a tree.

A vine.

One of Casey's sling-traps.

Valerie suddenly discovered a quick way to get up into the tree—and fast.

She ran toward it.

The natives were there now. She could see the whites of their eyes as she looked behind her.

The boars were there now. She could see their dirty, yellow teeth glistening in the darkness.

She was there now. She took off in a high jump that landed her directly in the center of the trap. In an instant, she felt her feet being swept up underneath her and her upper body cascading down. Her head brushed close to the jungle floor as she swung straight up.

The force of air was fierce and she was going so fast she couldn't possibly locate a stable branch to grab onto. She kept going up.

Like a rocket during blastoff, she pierced the air and broke through the tree branches. She was slowing slightly, and she could make out branch sizes. She reached out for a medium-sized one and missed.

She reached out for the next one, but retracted her hand when it talked.

"Hallo, Val! Extra tight!" it said. It was Casey! She saw his glowing smile as she continued to fling through the foliage. He had planted that trap on purpose. He had saved her!

Valerie could barely keep her eyes open. There! Another large branch! Reach for it...now! Valerie reached forward and would have had it, but she heard something that made her give up the opportunity.

Tss-ss-ss-ss-ss-ss-ss...

A rattlesnake?! No! It was the SuperCopter! Valerie broke through the treetops, bursting into the fresh, clean night air. Stars sparkled all around her and the deep crimson and purple sunset nearly stole her breath away. She had reached the top of her flight and the force of gravity was ready to pull her back down. But before gravity was able to take its hold, Valerie grabbed on tightly to a large, straight metal bar cruising past her. The suddenness of her change in direction jolted her whole being.

The SuperCopter jarred with the sudden, added weight, but its pilot quickly steadied it out. Rapper looked out the SuperCopter's window and saw Valerie dangling from its sturdy landing bar. His eyes grew big in shock and his jaw dropped like a cartoon character's. He'd been flying over slowly, praying, following the Lord's direction, fishing for a clue...little did he expect the prize catch!

"Valerie?!?!" he mouthed from inside. She nodded, feeling warm tears roll down her cheeks and blow away into the night. The vine at her feet snapped free and Rapper swung open the side door. Valerie pulled herself up with only a little difficulty and closed the door.

"Ha-ha!" Rapper shouted, setting the SuperCopter into autopilot mode and throwing his arms around Valerie. He grabbed her as tight as a bear and she returned the hug. She was crying heavily now, with joy bursting up from her heart. He thumped on her back playfully, unable to contain his joy.

"I made it...I made it..." she said over and over. "I knew you wouldn't stop looking for me."

They pulled back for a moment and Valerie looked at Rapper's wide, heart-warming smile.

"You look awful," he admitted, smiling big. Valerie laughed and cried again, so thankful to be rescued. It had looked impossible, but the Lord had made a way.

Rapper attended to the controls and Valerie looked through her tears into the night sky ahead. The darkness wasn't threatening. The night wasn't scary. For within her, Valerie found a light far brighter than any darkness could ever overcome. She had found her freedom. She had escaped from Jungle Island.

Three days had passed since Valerie's adventure on Jungle Island. Of course, when she and Rapper landed, her parents cried and laughed and hugged her tight. They celebrated by roasting up the biggest wild boar they could find on Calypso Island. They sang and listened to Valerie's stories about the mysterious island, the Manwans, her brush with wild animals, and her new friend Casey.

Valerie thought about him as she lay in the soft bed in her room. Rapper was staying in a hut with friends of the family and her parents were asleep. The island was quiet and Valerie could hear insects chirping outside her window. The sky was a deep, dark bluish-purple, speckled with twinkling stars and a beaming, whole moon.

Her fear of the night was gone. Her life totally and thoroughly belonged to the Lord. A light breeze brushed a wisp of her dark, brown hair away from her face as she thought about Casey and the Manwans. They were ready to take her life...in fact, they had tried to...but she still felt a burning compassion in her heart for them. God still loved them. Maybe one day they would see that their god, Guphigai, was nothing but wood and clay, sealed with fear.

Valerie found herself praying for her enemies, praying that someone someday could reach them in a way they would understand. She prayed that someone would be able to speak to them, completely unafraid. She prayed that her words about her God would live on in the tribe. She knew the Word of the Lord could not be stopped. It was alive and working constantly where she sent it.

She also prayed for Casey, her new friend. The Manwan who was not a Manwan. The Manwan who was not afraid. The Manwan who helped save her life. She prayed that he would find a way to escape Jungle Island, too. Because it could be done—Valerie was living proof. She closed her eyes. Like a whisper, Valerie pretended she could hear his voice.

"Hallo, Val."

Valerie smiled as she dreamed. The memory was sweet.

"Hello, Valerie Rivera."

Valerie frowned. *That* sounded like the Manwan leader...She refocused her thoughts back to Casey's voice.

"Hello, Valerie Rivera." Humph. Valerie pushed aside the voice and opened up her eyes to look at the sparkling night sky again. But it wasn't there. In its place stood a huge, dark figure. The Manwan leader. He was in her room. Valerie opened her mouth to scream, but a small hand shot from the other side of her bed and covered it. Valerie looked at the body attached to the hand. It was Casey.

Valerie sat up and Casey let go. "Casey!" she shouted, hugging him with one arm. She held the bedcover close to her with the other, keeping herself warm with it over her nightgown.

"Shhh..." Casey hushed, putting a finger to his lips. Valerie looked at the Manwan leader and back at Casey.

"What are you two doing here?" she asked. She had a right to know. It was her bedroom.

"I asked Casey to bring me here so I could learn more about the God above all gods," Honcho responded, timidly.

"I don't understand," Valerie admitted, shaking her head. "First you try to kill me and now you want—"

"You were the One, Valerie Rivera."

"The One? I don't...what do you mean, 'The One'?"

The Manwan leader knelt down, wide-eyed beside her bed.

"Manwan legend says that long ago a prophet came to our tribe. He told us that one day a messenger would come and bring us the Truth. He told us to watch for the messenger—and to watch for a sign."

Valerie reflected back to the arched doorway to the Manwan temple. She remembered the carving of the figure. Above him was an arrow pointing to the sky. Above that was a starburst...a symbol of the sign he would leave. Valerie shook her head in disbelief. It was hard for her to imagine that she—a young girl—could be the fulfillment of an ancient prophecy.

"But, sir," she addressed Honcho, "how do you know it's me? Others—"

"The prophecy specifically states that the messenger would be one who would soar through the air like an arrow. And my people have told me the story of your escape. They had you surrounded...but you went straight up into the air."

Valerie turned to Casey. "Yeah, but I was just caught in a tight-vine trap Casey made. I—"

"That doesn't change the prophecy, Valerie Rivera. It never stated how the One would soar, it just stated that he would."

Valerie looked at Casey and the Manwan leader blank-faced. Then she said, "But wasn't there supposed to be a—"

"Sign," Honcho interrupted. "Yes. And you left us more than one of those." Valerie shook her head. She felt groggy, like it was all a dream. The Manwan leader continued. "You were not burned. Guphigai was."

Casey spoke up. "And..." He held out his left hand. Valerie's lip quivered. He no longer wore the bandage with the skull. He didn't need to. His hand and thumb were completely smooth, completely full of color again, completely healed. "Cayseilauphlan no sick," he said, proudly. "Cayseilauphlan see Val no fear and so Cayseilauphlan serve Val's God. Val's God heal Cayseilauphlan."

"Then it's true," she whispered, staring blankly. She *was* the fulfillment of an ancient prophecy. She didn't understand how it had all happened, but she had ended up in the right place at the right time. And because she was not afraid—not ashamed of the gospel—God used her. She was still young...but God used her to reach a whole world of people. She was able to give them seeds of Truth that would live on for generations to come.

▲ ▲ ▲

"Yo! Val!" Rapper's head popped through her bedroom window. She was startled awake and the sunshine framing his head pierced her eyes. "What? You're not up yet."

Valerie tried to yawn discreetly, but she couldn't hold her mouth closed. "Sor...ry," she breathed out with her yawn. "What? What's happening?"

Rapper looked like he was a little embarrassed. "Well, I didn't mean to wake you up."

"It's all right. You know, I had the strangest dream last night."

"Yeah?"

"Yeah. I dreamed the Manwan leader came with Casey and told me that I was the fulfillment of an ancient prophecy."

"Now why don't I have dreams like that?"

Valerie smirked. "Because you didn't spend your first few days of vacation running from killer natives."

"Oh, yeah. So that's it? That's how it ended?"

"No. They swore me to secrecy. They said it would take time to share the Truth with all the Manwans. They have a lot of tradition with their Goofyguy god, you know."

"Of course."

"So I gave them some Bibles and stuff to get them started. They said they'd contact my dad when their people were open enough to receiving more. But it was a great start. It was a powerfully sown seed."

"Sounds like a great dream."

Valerie sat up and slipped her legs out of the bed. They dangled over the floor. "Keep praying for them." Rapper took it as his cue to leave.

"Well, I just came to see if you wanted to join me in calling Commander Kellie. They've had some time to analyze the information about our crash. See who shot at us and stuff. Thought you might want to hear what it was that caused us to go down."

"That's all right," she responded. "Go ahead without me. I think I'm gonna take my time getting ready today, then I'm gonna hit the beach. I'm ready to take things just a tad bit slower."

"'K," he said, slapping the window frame. "Catch ya."

Valerie listened to his feet tap against the ground as he walked away. Rapper was a good friend. She pushed the covers aside and brushed at her long, dark-blue nightgown. Today was going to be good day. She could finally relax. No lightning storms, no tropical snakes, no wild boars, no caiman crocodiles, no false gods, no sacrificial bonfires, no threatening natives.

She dropped her feet to the floor, but withdrew them when she hit her shoes. Strange. She didn't remember placing them there. Then her eyebrows drew together as her mouth went dry. It was her pair of cross trainers. Not her one cross trainer and Casey's homemade leaf sandal. It was her *pair.* Both were there. The one she returned with, and the one she had lost in the boar trap.

Valerie looked around the room for indications that anyone had been there...but there weren't any. No footprints, nothing out of place. Nothing indicating that anyone else had been near. Except the shoe.

Valerie swallowed and then smiled contentedly. Maybe someone *had* visited her in the middle of the night. Maybe it wasn't just a dream. Valerie slowly rubbed her finger along the shoe's soft, leather texture. No, there was no "maybe" about it. Valerie realized her dream had come true. Someone else, just for a brief meeting, had also escaped from Jungle Island.

Rapper flipped on a communication panel in the SuperCopter and in a matter of moments he had a direct link to Superkid Academy. Commander Kellie had an encryption code immediately placed on the transmission, which Rapper knew meant there must be trouble.

"Valerie's taking it easy today," Rapper said as a greeting.

"Hello, Superkid," the commander responded. "Well, I can't blame her. She's been through a lot. But God is faithful. He's brought her through in victory."

Rapper nodded and smiled. "So did you guys find anything out about those shots that were taken at us?"

"Indeed." Commander Kellie's face on the view screen moved down to look at something. *Probably some kind of report,* Rapper reasoned. "We found there was an unusual energy signature near your craft for quite some time."

"So someone *was* following us! They must have been jamming our radar so we couldn't see them. Any idea who it was?"

"The answer's not going to surprise you."

In unison, Rapper and Commander Kellie voiced, "NME."

"But why shoot at us?" Rapper demanded. "We weren't doing anything but going on vacation!"

"That's what I plan to find out," Commander Kellie assured the Superkid.

"Don't tell me..."

The Commander's attractive face smiled through the view screen. Her eyebrows jumped up and down when she announced, "I tracked them."

"That's why you're the *commander,*" Rapper said with a chuckle.

"Since the area isn't as technologically advanced as most, it was easy. Once I identified the signal, I laid in a relay which traced it back to an NME Frightcraft. Our sources tell me there are only four NME Frightcrafts currently in operation. And only one was out of port this weekend—one piloted by NME agent #2039, a Miss Mashela—"

"Knavery," Rapper finished. "Yeah, I've heard of her. She's got quite a reputation. Weapons specialist, covert maneuvers training—secret agent extraordinaire. I don't envy the army that's going to go after her."

"I'm sending Alex."

"Alex who?"

"Rapper—I'm sending *our* Alex. He's the only one available for the job. Paul and Missy are nearly 1,000 miles away and you're even farther. She'll have disappeared by the time any of you could get back. Alex is it. And I believe he can do it. All he has to do is keep track of her.

Then, once we get some reinforcements, we can bring her in for questioning."

Rapper knew better than to argue with the commander. She knew what she was doing. Besides, she was right. All he had to do was track her. There wouldn't be too much trouble in that, would there?

"Well, I'll be interested in knowing what happens."

"I'll keep in touch. Meanwhile, have a good couple more days vacation. And pray for Alex. He'll have his hands full."

To be continued...

The **last thing** Alex remembered
was tracking down an NME agent.

In fact, that's the *only* **thing** he remembers.

Look for *Commander Kellie and the Superkids*
novel #4—

In Pursuit of the Enemy

by Christopher P.N. Maselli

Prayer for Salvation

Father God, I believe that Jesus is Your Son and that You raised Him from the dead for me. Jesus, I give my life to You. Right now, I make You the Lord of my life and choose to follow You forever. I love You and I know You love me. Thank You, Jesus, for giving me a new life. Thank You for coming into my heart and being my Savior. I am a child of God! Amen.

About the Author

Christopher P.N. Maselli is the author of the *Commander Kellie and the Superkids* series. He also writes the bimonthly children's magazine, *Shout! The Voice of Victory for Kids,* and has contributed to the *Commander Kellie and the Superkids*sm movies.

Originally from Iowa and a graduate of Oral Roberts University, Chris now lives with his wife, Gena, in Fort Worth, Texas, where he is actively involved in the children's ministry at his local church. When he's not writing, he enjoys in-line skating, playing computer games and collecting Legos.

Other Books Available

Baby Praise Board Book
Noah's Ark Coloring Book
The Shout! Super-Activity Book

Commander Kellie and the Superkids Books:

The SWORD Adventure Book
Commander Kellie and the Superkids
Preteen Novels by Christopher P.N. Maselli

#1 *The Mysterious Presence*
#2 *The Quest for the Second Half*
#3 *Escape From Jungle Island*
#4 *In Pursuit of the Enemy*

World Offices
of Kenneth Copeland Ministries

For more information about KCM and a free
catalog, please write the office nearest you:

Kenneth Copeland Ministries
Fort Worth, Texas 76192-0001

Kenneth Copeland
Locked Bag 2600
Mansfield Delivery Centre
QUEENSLAND 4122
AUSTRALIA

Kenneth Copeland
Post Office Box 15
BATH
BA1 1GD
ENGLAND

Kenneth Copeland
Private Bag X 909
FONTAINEBLEAU
2032
REPUBLIC OF SOUTH AFRICA

Kenneth Copeland
Post Office Box 378
Surrey
BRITISH COLUMBIA
V3T 5B6
CANADA

UKRAINE
L'VIV 290000
Post Office Box 84
Kenneth Copeland Ministries
L'VIV 290000
UKRAINE

We're Here for You!

Shout! ...The dynamic magazine just for kids!

Shout! The Voice of Victory for Kids is a Bible-charged, action-packed, bimonthly magazine available FREE to kids everywhere! Featuring *Wichita Slim* and *Commander Kellie and the Superkids*, *Shout!* is filled with colorful adventure comics, challenging games and puzzles, exciting short stories, solve-it-yourself mysteries and much more!!

Stand up, sign up and get ready to *Shout!*

Believer's Voice of Victory Television Broadcast

Join Kenneth and Gloria Copeland, and the *Believer's Voice of Victory* broadcasts, Monday through Friday and on Sunday each week, and learn how faith in God's Word can take your life from ordinary to extraordinary. This is some of the best teaching you'll ever hear, designed to get you where you want to be—*on top!*

You can catch the *Believer's Voice of Victory* broadcast on your local, cable or satellite channels.

*Check your local listings for times and stations in your area.

Believer's Voice of Victory Magazine

Enjoy inspired teaching and encouragement from Kenneth and Gloria Copeland each month in the *Believer's Voice of Victory* magazine. Also included are real-life testimonies of God's miraculous power and divine intervention into the lives of people just like you!

It's more than just a magazine—it's a ministry.

If you or some of your friends would like to receive a FREE subscription to *Shout!,* just send each kid's name, date of birth and complete address to:

Kenneth Copeland Ministries
Fort Worth, Texas 76192-0001
Or call:
1-800-359-0075
(9 a.m.-5 p.m. CT)

The Harrison House Vision

Proclaiming the truth and the power
Of the Gospel of Jesus Christ
With excellence;

Challenging Christians to
Live victoriously,
Grow spiritually,
Know God intimately.